PLOUGHSHAI

Winter 2007–08 · Vol. 33,

GUEST EDITOR
Philip Levine

INTERIM EDITOR-IN-CHIEF
DeWitt Henry

MANAGING DIRECTOR
Robert Arnold

FICTION EDITOR
Margot Livesey

POETRY EDITOR
John Skoyles

ASSOCIATE FICTION EDITOR
Maryanne O'Hara

FOUNDING PUBLISHER
Peter O'Malley

PLOUGHSHARES, a journal of new writing, is guest-edited serially by prominent writers who explore different and personal visions, aesthetics, and literary circles. PLOUGHSHARES is published in April, August, and December at Emerson College, 120 Boylston Street, Boston, MA 02116-4624. Telephone: (617) 824-8753. Web address: pshares.org.

ASSISTANT EDITOR: Laura van den Berg. EDITORIAL ASSISTANTS: Grace Schauer and Kat Setzer. HEAD READER: Jay Baron Nicorvo. PROOFREADER: Megan Weireter.

POETRY READERS: Kathleen Rooney, Simeon Berry, Grace Schauer, Elisa Gabbert, Heather Madden, Autumn McClintock, Liz Bury, David Semanki, Matt Summers, Chris Tonelli, Julia Story, Maria Halovanic, Jennifer Kohl, Pepe Abola, and Meredith Devney. FICTION READERS: Kat Setzer, Kathleen Rooney, Simeon Berry, Chip Cheek, Chris Helmuth, Leslie Busler, Steve Himmer, Eson Kim, Wendy Wunder, Matt Salesses, Shannon Derby, Cam Terwilliger, Kat Gonso, Dan Medeiros, Sage Marsters, Emily Ekle, Sara Whittleton, James Charlesworth, Hannah Bottomy, Jim Scott, Patricia Reed, Vanessa Carlisle, Leslie Cauldwell, Jason Roeder, and Gregg Rosenblum. NON-FICTION READER: Katherine Newman.

SUBSCRIPTIONS (ISSN 0048-4474): $24 for one year (3 issues), $46 for two years (6 issues); $27 a year for institutions. Add $12 a year for international ($10 for Canada).

UPCOMING: Spring 2008, a poetry and fiction issue edited by B. H. Fairchild, will appear in April 2008. Fall 2008, a fiction issue edited by James Alan McPherson, will appear in August 2008.

SUBMISSIONS: Reading period is from August 1 to March 31 (postmark and online dates). All submissions sent from April to July are returned unread. Please see page xxx for editorial and submission policies.

Back-issue, classroom-adoption, and bulk orders may be placed directly through PLOUGHSHARES. Microfilms of back issues may be obtained from University Microfilms. PLOUGHSHARES is also available as CD-ROM and full-text products from EBSCO, H.W. Wilson, ProQuest, and the Gale Group. Indexed in M.L.A. Bibliography, American Humanities Index, Index of American Periodical Verse, Book Review Index. Full publisher's index is online at pshares.org. The views and opinions expressed in this journal are solely those of the authors. All rights for individual works revert to the authors upon publication. PLOUGHSHARES receives support from the National Endowment for the Arts and the Massachusetts Cultural Council.

Retail distribution by Ingram Periodicals and Source Interlink. Printed in the U.S.A. by Edwards Brothers.

© 2008 by Emerson College   ISBN 978-1-933058-08-5

CONTENTS

Winter 2007–08

Cover art:
Untitled by
Michael Mazur
Drawing with mixed media, 2004

Ploughshares Patrons

This nonprofit publication would not be possible without the
support of our readers and the generosity of the following
individuals and organizations.

COUNCIL: $3,000 for two lifetime subscriptions and
acknowledgement in the journal for three years.
PATRON: $1,000 for a lifetime subscription and
acknowledgement in the journal for two years.
FRIEND: $500 for a lifetime subscription and
acknowledgement in the journal for one year.

Introduction

Looking back at the table of contents of an earlier issue of *Ploughshares* that I guest-edited some twenty years ago, I was surprised by how few of the writers were then discoveries for me. Two certainly were. Their poems had almost nothing in common: her three poems were straightforward & hard-edged; the details came out of her working-class life in Detroit & elsewhere. The other's poem was far more oblique & shrewd, but his voice no less authoritative. I was deeply moved by the poems of both of them—reading them now all these years later I'm even more impressed by my editorship, if that's possible. They were a highpoint of my working on that issue. There's nothing quite like discovering someone out there you never heard of but you know in an instant is the real thing.

I ask myself why is it that in the last two decades I've seen almost no poems by the first, while the other, Dean Young, has gone on to considerable success and deserved recognition. (I met him for the second time in May at a meeting of the American Academy of Arts & Letters, where he was receiving an award for his body of work.) Luck, good health (often a form of luck), perseverance, character, the profound need simply to make poems & keep making them? It could be that some writers early in their careers figure out a wise use of their literary capital & others don't. Of course fashions change, & a poet's work can come into or out of fashion through no effort on his or her part. (I think if I were starting out now no editor in his right mind would publish me.) It is also possible that the first poet has stayed true to her engagement with poetry & merely grown tired of the whole process of publication & acclimation, & that she possesses a closet of superb unpublished poems the writing of which were satisfaction enough. I hope that is the case, for her poems that appeared in this magazine are like no one else's. Anyone who has written poetry in America—that is tried to make a life of it—can understand how a poet can become disgusted with everything that relates to "a career." A weekend at an AWP annual conference can drive a sane person to studying rainfall in the Kalahari, or selling shoes in Saginaw.

As I push on into old age—I'll be eighty a month after this issue appears—I wonder more & more how & why some of us turn away from poetry, & others—like me—keep writing for better or worse. This essential puzzle reminds me of a wonderful song I once heard Lightnin' Hopkins sing at a retirement center here in Fresno. (I'd gone to the place to hear Hopkins & not to retire.) In this song, there was a line that was repeated again & again as though to authenticate itself: "I just keep scrubbin' at the same old thing." At the time, back in the late seventies, Hopkins was much younger than I am now, but he wasn't young. I was young enough then to think the song was about fucking, but now it strikes me that the song may have been about enduring as whatever one is, & getting what pleasure one can from simply persisting. For all I know, Hopkins did his own laundry & was being totally literal. Even a great blues singer's clothes get dirty after a time & require laundering. Dirty clothes or not, Lightnin' "kept scrubbin'" at the same old thing, that is he persisted in his craft & art, & remained—as one critic wrote—"a walking embodiment of the blues" right up until his death in his early seventies.

In poetry, for many years my model has been Thomas Hardy, who, for me, came into his greatness as a poet in old age. *Jude the Obscure,* published when he was sixty-five, received such a ghastly reception that Hardy, I've read, turned away from the writing of novels. But of course he kept writing. The curious thing is that the poems he wrote in his seventies & eighties are far less bleak in their vision than that final novel. Indeed, there are moments of utter triumph, poems so perfectly wrought & so at peace with the death that would soon be his, that one wonders if, after all the pain & all the losses of his difficult life, he did not wander into some small region of redemption. This man who had seemed so distant from a life-changing epiphany or a vision of cosmic beauty writes in his final book—published posthumously & completed just before he turned eighty-nine—one of the great lyrical & triumphant poems in our language:

Proud Songsters

The thrushes sing as the sun is going,
And the finches whistle in ones and pairs,
And as it gets dark loud nightingales
        In bushes
Pipe, as they can when April wears,
        As if all time were theirs.

These are brand-new birds of twelve-months growing,
Which a year ago, or less than twain,
No finches were, nor nightingale,
        Nor thrushes,
But only particles of grain,
        And earth, and air, and rain.

A great artist in his last days still in possession of perfect mastery over our magnificent language. It's truly inspiring to see an artist in his final years capable of such technical wizardry & emotional power. Other examples come to mind: Monet, Picasso, Matisse, Sophocles, & in our own time Pablo Casals & Stanley Kunitz. Gaudi was just realizing his true greatness as a visionary architect when in his mid-seventies he was hit by a streetcar. He had given up both smoking & drinking, & it had been decades since he'd chased after young women. With some luck, exercise, & good nutrition he might have completed his great masterpiece, the Sagrada Familia. Is there any likelihood that I could join these giants? (Or that you could, for that matter?) I wouldn't bet on it. In my sixty-five years of stumbling toward verse I've never done anything to suggest such mastery was alive or even dormant within me. But I also know how monumentally stubborn I am, & how deeply I believe in scrubbin'. If clean clothes is all I get, so be it. One of the glories of writing poetry is just how badly & how often you can fail & still believe in your right & need to make poems; if you have any success at all, it is utterly thrilling.

from The Condition

Summer comes late to Massachusetts. The gray spring is frosty, unhurried: wet snow on the early plantings, a cold lesson for optimistic gardeners, for those who have not learned. Chimneys smoke until Memorial Day. Then, all at once, the ceiling lifts. The sun fires, scorching the muddy ground.

At the Cape, the rhythm is eternal, unchanging. Icy tides smash the beaches. Then cold ones. Then cool. The bay lies warming in the long days. Blue-lipped children brave the surf.

They opened the house the third week in June—the summer of the Bicentennial, and of Paulette's thirty-fifth birthday. She drove from Concord to the train station in Boston, where her sister was waiting, then happily surrendered the wheel. Martine was better in traffic, which was not surprising. She'd been better in school, on the tennis court; for two years she'd been the top-ranked Singles player at Wellesley. Now, at thirty-eight, Martine was a *career girl*, still a curiosity in those days, at least in her family. She worked for an advertising agency on Madison Avenue—doing what precisely, Paulette was not certain. Her sister lived alone in New York City, a prospect she found terrifying. But Martine had always been fearless.

The station wagon was packed with Paulette's children and their belongings. Billy and Gwen, fourteen and twelve, rode in the back seat, a pile of beach towels between them. Scotty, nine and so excited about the Cape that he was nearly insufferable, had been banished to the rear.

"God, would you look at this?" Martine downshifted, shielding her eyes from the sun. The traffic had slowed to a crawl, big American engines idling loudly, the stagnant air rich with fumes. The Sagamore Bridge was still half a mile away. "It gets worst every year. Too many goddamned cars."

A giggle from the back seat, Gwen probably. Paulette frowned. She disapproved of cursing, especially by women, especially in front of children.

"And how was the birthday?" Martine asked. "I can't believe *la petite Paulette* is thirty-five. Did you do anything special?"

Her tone was casual; she may not have known it was a tender subject. Like no birthday before, this one had unsettled Paulette. The number seemed somehow significant. She'd been married fifteen years, but only now did she feel like a matron.

"Frank took me into town. We had a lovely dinner." She didn't mention that he'd also reserved a room at the Ritz, a presumptuous gesture that irritated her. Like all Frank's presents, it was a gift less for her than for himself.

"Will he grace us with his presence this year?"

Paulette ignored the facetious tone. "Next weekend, maybe, if he can get away. If not, then definitely for the Fourth."

"He's teaching this summer?"

"No," Paulette said carefully. "He's in the lab." She always felt defensive discussing Frank's work with Martine, who refused to understand that he wasn't only a teacher but also a scientist. (*Molecular developmental biology,* Paulette said when anyone asked what he studied. This usually discouraged further questions.) Frank's lab worked year-round, seven days a week. Last year, busy writing a grant proposal, he hadn't come to the Cape at all. Martine seemed to take this as a personal slight, though she'd never seemed to enjoy his company. *He's an academic,* Martine said testily. *He gets the summers off. Isn't that the whole point?* It was clear from the way she pronounced the word what she thought of *academics.* Martine saw in Frank the same flaws Paulette did: his obsession with his work, his smug delight in his own intellect. She simply didn't forgive him as Paulette—as women generally—always had. Frank had maintained for years that Martine hated him, a claim Paulette dismissed: *Don't be silly. She's very fond of you.* (Why tell such a lie? Because Martine was family, and she *ought* to be fond of Frank. Paulette had firm ideas, back then, of how things ought to be.)

In Truro the air was cooler. Finally the traffic thinned. Martine turned off the main route and onto the No Name Road, a narrow lane that had only recently been paved. Their father had taught the girls, as children, to recite the famous line from Thoreau: *Cape Cod is the bared and bended arm of Massachusetts. The shoulder is at Buzzard's Bay; the elbow at Cape Mallebarre; the wrist at*

Truro; the sandy fist at Provincetown. Remembering this, Paulette felt a stab of tenderness for her father. Everett Drew had made his living as a patent attorney; he viewed ideas as property of the most precious kind. In his mind, Thoreau was the property of New England, of Concord, Massachusetts; perhaps even particularly of the Drews.

"How's Daddy feeling?" she asked Martine, who'd just returned from a visit to Florida. Their brother Roy had convinced Everett to retire, then parked both parents in a condominium in Palm Beach. Paulette visited when she could, but this was no substitute for Sunday dinners at her parents' house, the gentle rhythm of family life, broken now, gone forever.

"He misses you," said Martine. "But he made do with me."

Paulette blinked. She was often blindsided by how acerbic her sister could be, how in the midst of a pleasant conversation Martine could deliver a zinger that stopped her cold: the backhanded compliment, the ripe apple with the razor inside. When they were children she'd often crept up behind Paulette and pulled her hair for no reason, so it wasn't her adult life, alone in a big city, that had made Martine prickly. She had always been that way.

They turned off the No Name Road onto a rutted path. It being June, the lane was rugged, two deep tire tracks grown in between with grass. By the end of summer it would be worn smooth. The Captain's House was set squarely at the end of it, three rambling stories covered in shingle. A deep porch wrapped around three sides.

As she had every summer of her life, Paulette sprang out of the car first, forgetting for a moment her children in the back seat, Scotty whiny and fidgeting in the rear. For a split second, she was a girl again, taking inventory, checking that all was as she'd left it the year before. Each member of the family performed some version of this ritual. Her brother Roy rushed first to the boathouse, Martine to the rocky beach. But it was the cottage itself that called to Paulette, the familiar stairs and hallways, the odd corners and closets and built-in cupboards where she'd hidden as a child—the tiniest of the Drew cousins, a little Houdini—in games of hide and seek. The Captain's House, the family called it, in memory of Clarence Hubbard Drew, Paulette's great, great grandfather, a sailor and whaler. Clarence had hired a distinguished architect, a distant cousin of Ralph Waldo Emerson. The house had the graceful lines of the shingle style; it was built for comfort rather than grandeur. A house with wide doors and windows, a house meant to be flung open. On summer nights, a cross breeze whipped through the first floor, a cool tunnel of ocean-smelling air.

Paulette stood a moment staring at the façade, the house's only architectural flourish: three diamond-shaped windows placed just above the front door. The windows were set in staggered fashion, rising on the diagonal like stairs, a fact Paulette, as a child, had found significant. She was the lowest window, her brother Roy the highest. The middle window was Martine.

She noticed, then, a car parked in the sandy driveway that curved behind the house. Her brother's family had already arrived.

"Will you look at that?" said Martine, coming up behind her. "Anne has a new Mercedes."

Paulette, herself, would not have not have noticed. In such matters, she deferred to her husband, who was partial to Saabs and Volvos.

Martine smirked. "Roy has come up in the world."

"Martine, hush." Paulette refused to let her sister spoil this moment, the exhilarating first minutes of summer, the joyful return.

They unloaded the car: brown paper bags from the grocery store in Orleans, the oblong case that held Gwen's telescope. Tied to the roof were suitcases and Billy's new ten-speed, an early birthday present. Martine stood on her toes to unfasten them.

"Let me," said Billy, untying the ropes easily, his fingers thick as a man's. He had sailed since he was a toddler and was a specialist at complicated knots. Not yet fourteen, he towered over his mother. He had been a beautiful child, and would be an exceptionally handsome man; but that summer Paulette found him difficult to look at. His new maturity was everywhere: his broad shoulders, his coarsening voice, the blond peach fuzz on his upper lip. Normal, natural, necessary changes—yet somehow shocking, embarrassing to them both.

They followed the gravel path, loaded down with groceries, and nudged open the screen door. A familiar scent greeted them, a smell Paulette's memory labeled *Summer.* It was the smell of her

own childhood, complex and irreducible, though she could iden-
tify a few components: sea air, Murphy's Oil Soap, cedar closets
that had stood closed the long winter, the aged wood macerating
in its own resins, waiting for the family to return.

"These go upstairs?" Billy asked, standing in the doorway with
two suitcases.

"Yes, dear." She put down the groceries in the airless kitchen,
wondering why her sister-in-law hadn't thought to open the windows. Billy carried the bags upstairs. The house had nine bed-
rooms, a few so small that only a child could sleep there without
claustrophobia. The third-floor rooms, stifling in summertime,
were used only as a last resort. The same was true of the tiny
alcove off the kitchen, which had once been the cook's quarters.
Since her marriage, Paulette had slept in a sunny front bedroom—Fanny's Room, according to the homemade wooden plac-
ard hanging on the door. Fanny Porter had been a school chum of
Paulette's grandmother; she'd been dead thirty years or more, but
thanks to a long-ago Drew cousin, who'd made the signs as a
rainy-day project at the behest of some governess, the room
would forever be known as Fanny's.

The sleeping arrangements at the house were the same each
year. Roy and Anne took the Captain's Quarters at the rear of the
house, the biggest room with the best view. Frank, if he came,
would grouse about this, but Paulette didn't mind. *Someone* had
to sleep in the Captain's Quarters, to take her father's place at the
dinner table. That it was Roy, the eldest son, seemed correct, the
natural order of things. Correct, too, that Gwen shared prime
accommodations, along with Roy's two daughters, on the sleeping
porch, where Martine and Paulette and their Drew cousins had
slept as girls. The porch was screened on three sides; even on the
hottest nights, ocean breezes swept through. Across the hall was
the Lilac Room, named for its sprigged wallpaper, and Martine's
favorite, the Whistling Room, whose old windows hummed like a
teakettle when the wind came in from the west. Billy and Scotty
took the wood-paneled downstairs bedroom—The Bunk
House—where Roy and the boy cousins had once slept. It was this
sameness that Paulette treasured, the summer ritual unchanging,
the illusion of permanence.

That afternoon, they packed a picnic basket and piled into the car. Sailors Beach, their own bit of coastline, was rough and rocky. Martine could spend whole days there, paddling the kayak and clambering over boulders; but Paulette and the children preferred the National Seashore, with its endless swath of sand. For this brief trip, Paulette took the wheel, with a confidence she never felt in Boston. She loved driving the Cape roads, familiar, gently winding; she could have driven them in her sleep. Scotty claimed the passenger seat after a tussle with his brother. *Billy, darling, just let him have it, will you?* she pleaded. After sitting in the car all morning, her youngest was wild as a cat. In this state, Paulette found him ungovernable and rather frightening. Her only hope was to turn him loose outdoors, where he could blow off some steam.

She sat on a blanket in the shade of an umbrella, *My Antonia* lying open in her lap. She'd brought *Lord of the Flies* for Billy, who would read his daily chapter without complaint; and *Little Women* for Gwen, who would not. Paulette believed firmly in summer reading, and because she'd loved the Alcott books as a girl, she couldn't fathom why Gwen did not. Seeing Orchard House had been the greatest thrill of Paulette's twelve year-old life. "That's where Louisa grew up, right here in Concord," she'd told her daughter. This proved to be insufficient enticement. After a week of cajoling, Gwen still hadn't opened the book.

Paulette shifted slightly, moving nearer to the umbrella. Its positioning had been the subject of much discussion. Her sister-in-law Anne, coated in baby oil, wanted as much sun as possible; Paulette needed complete shade. She had been cautioned by visiting her parents in Palm Beach, a town populated by leathery retirees who lived their lives poolside, their bodies lined in places she'd never imagined could wrinkle.

Martine stood back from the discussion, laughing at them both.

"You make quite a picture," she said. Paulette wore a large straw hat and, over her swimsuit, striped beach pajamas, their wide legs flapping like flags in the wind. Anne wore a white bikini more suited to a teenager, for maximum sun exposure. The bikini was made of triangles. Two inverted ones made up the bottom. Two smaller ones, attached by string, formed the top.

Paulette had known Anne most of her life. Roy had met her his first semester at Harvard, when Paulette was eleven, and she had fallen in love with Anne too. They were as close as sisters, closer, certainly, than Paulette and Martine. Paulette admired her sister, but couldn't confide in her. Martine seemed to find the world so easy. She had no patience for someone who did not.

Anne lit a cigarette. After giving birth to her second daughter, she'd taken up smoking to regain her figure. Charlotte was twelve now, and Anne, so thin her ribs showed, still smoked.

They watched as Martine joined the boys in the surf. She was expert at what she called body surfing. Martine waiting for her moment, her slick head bobbing. Martine diving fearlessly into the waves.

"You can relax now," Anne said, chuckling. "Auntie Lifeguard is on duty."

"That's the problem. She'll get them all killed." Paulette shifted slightly, to avoid the streaming smoke. "When is Roy coming?"

"Friday morning. He's dying to put the boat in the water." Anne rolled onto her stomach, then untied her bikini top. "Can you grease my back?"

Paulette took the baby oil she offered and squirted it into her hands. Anne's skin felt hot and papery, dry to the touch.

"I don't know if Frank will make it this year," said Paulette. *I don't know if I want him to,* she nearly added. At home they coexisted peacefully, more or less, though Frank spent so much time at the lab that they rarely saw each other. At the Cape, they'd have to spend whole days together. *What will we talk about all day?* she wondered. *What on earth will we do?*

She knew what Frank would want to do. His sexual demands overwhelmed her. If he'd asked less often, she might have felt bad about refusing; but if Frank had his way, they would make love every night. After fifteen years of marriage, it seemed excessive. Paulette sometimes wondered whether other couples did it so often, but she had no one to ask. Anne didn't shrink from personal questions, but she was Roy's wife. Certain things, Paulette truly didn't want to know.

Married sex: the familiar circuit of words and caresses and sensations, shuffled perhaps, but in the end always the same. The repetition wore on her. Each night when Frank reached for her she felt a hot flicker of irritation, then tamped it down. She willed herself to welcome him, to forget every hurt and disappointment, to hold herself open to all he was and wasn't. The effort exhausted her.

Years later, she would remember those marital nights with tenderness: for the brave young man Frank was, and for her young self, the wounded and stubborn girl. She'd had a certain idea about lovemaking, gleaned from Hollywood or God knew where, that a man's desire should be specific to her, triggered by her unique face or voice or—better—some intangible quality of her spirit; and that of all the women in the world, only she should be able to arouse him. And there lay the problem. Frank's passion, persistent and inexhaustible, seemed to have little to do with her. He came home from work bursting with it, though they hadn't seen or spoken to each other in many hours. *I've been thinking about this all day,* he sometimes whispered as he moved inside her.

This.

That one little word had the power to freeze her. Not, "I've been thinking about *you.*" But, "I've been thinking about *this.*"

It would seem comical later, how deeply this upset her. Like so many of her quarrels with Frank, it seemed ridiculous in hindsight. Once, early on, she had tried to explain it to Anne: *Frank loves sex. If he hadn't married me, he'd being having sex with someone else.*

So? Anne said.

For me it's different, Paulette insisted. *I love Frank. If I hadn't met him, I never would have had sex with anyone.*

It wasn't true, of course, but she wanted it to be. Her ideas were fixed, impossibly idealistic: Frank was the only man she could possibly have loved. Later this would seem a childish notion, but times had been different then. Paulette, her best friend Tricia Boone, her closest girlfriends at Wellesley—all had thought, or pretended to think, this way.

Frank, meanwhile, did not share in this illusion. She knew that he looked at other women. A certain type attracted him, large-breasted and voluptuous, a figure nothing like hers. When they went out together, to the symphony or the theater, Paulette found herself scanning the crowd, looking for the women he'd be drawn to. She was nearly always right; Frank proved it by ogling them right under her nose. He'd ruined her birthday dinner by flirting

shamelessly with the waitress. That night, at home—she declined
the hotel suite—he was surprised when she wouldn't let him
touch her. *What's the matter?* he asked, genuinely mystified. *Didn't
we have a good time?* She could have told him (but didn't) that
he'd made her feel invisible. But by then she didn't want to talk to
him. She didn't want him anywhere near her.

"Here come the girls," Anne said. Gwen and her cousins, Mimi
and Charlotte, had come in a separate car. Sixteen that spring,
Mimi had insisted on driving, proud of her brand new license.

The three girls trekked down the beach, towels draping their
shoulders. Mimi led the way—tall and coltish, with her father's
dark eyes and patrician nose. Charlotte, blonde and freckled,
resembled her mother. Gwen brought up the rear, her little legs
scrambling. She was the same age as Charlotte, but a head shorter.
Next to her cousins, she looked tiny as a doll.

Paulette watched them. "Charlotte certainly shot up this year,"
she observed.

"Yes, she did." Anne turned over onto her stomach. "It's done
wonders for her tennis game. I think she takes after Aunt Martine."

The girls laid their towels high on the dunes, away from their
mothers. The breeze carried their laughter as they stripped down
to swimsuits. Mimi wore a triangle bikini similar to her mother's,
but on her the effect was different. The rear triangle scarcely covered her rounded bottom. Her breasts, high and firm, peeked out
the sides of the top.

"My daughter," Anne said, laughing, as though she'd read
Paulette's mind. "Roy's going to have a heart attack when he sees
that bikini. If he had it his way, we'd never let her out of the
house."

Paulette watched her niece in wonderment. Mimi was the first
infant she'd ever held. In college then, she was overwhelmed by a
feeling she couldn't name. She'd loved everything about Mimi—
her baby smell, the dense, rounded weight of her. Holding her,
Paulette felt a knot low in her belly, an ache between her legs. The
feeling was nearly sexual, shocking in its intensity: *I want this. I
want one.*

She had adored her niece for sixteen years. Now she found it
impossible to look at the girl. Mimi with everything ahead of
her—love, discovery, every gift and possibility. Mimi's happiness

lay in the future; Paulette's, in the past. She was stunned by her own meanness. *I love this child,* she reminded herself. How ungenerous, how unseemly and futile to long for what was past.

"It's awful. I feel like a shriveled old hag." Anne lit another cigarette. "I have this beautiful daughter, and my whole body is sagging by the minute."

(Years later Paulette would marvel at the memory: how old they'd felt at thirty-five, how finished and depleted. *We were still young and beautiful,* she would realize far too late.)

"I'm not ready," Paulette said. "I don't want Gwen to grow up, not ever."

Anne chuckled. "I wouldn't start worrying yet. It looks like she has a long way to go."

They watched as Gwen charged into the surf. She wore a red tank suit with a pert ruffle around the hips. Her chest was still perfectly flat, her belly rounded like a little girl's.

Anne frowned. "She's twelve, right? Same as Charlotte?"

"Older, actually. She'll be thirteen in September."

For a long time, Anne was silent.

"Funny," she said finally, "how these things work."

That night they grilled hamburgers on the back porch. Paulette squelched a wave of panic as Martine showed Billy how to light the charcoal. "Relax, will you?" said Martine. "He's a big boy. He'll do fine."

"You're right, of course. Frank is always telling me not to hover." Paulette said this lightly, hiding her irritation. How like Martine to instruct her on child-rearing, an expert despite having no children of her own.

She spread a checkered cloth over the picnic table. This was her favorite part of the summer, these long, manless evenings. The children amused each other, leaving her free to drink wine with Anne and Martine. Had Frank and Roy been there—holding court on the patio, talking past each other, airing their opinions about nothing too interesting—the women would have retreated to the stuffy kitchen. They'd have turned the dinner into more work than was necessary, simply to have something to do.

That year Mimi had taken over the kitchen, mixing the salad, husking ears of corn. Watching her—fully dressed now—hand the platters to Billy, Paulette remembered the girl in her bikini, the miserable wash of envy she'd felt. The feeling had dissipated completely. As if sensing this, Mimi flashed her a shy smile, filling her with tenderness.

"What a helpful daughter you have," she told Anne.

"Billy's a good influence. Trust me, she never does this at home."

In that moment, warmed by the wine, Paulette was proud of the children they'd raised. In the fall, Billy would go away to Pearse; in a few years, he would bring home girlfriends, pretty girls like Mimi. He would fall in love. Watching him, she was struck by all that was delightful about this. Falling in love with Frank was the most thrilling thing that had ever happened to her. It seemed tragic to experience this just once, at the age of nineteen, and never again. Raising her children would give her a second chance at living those best years. A second and third and fourth chance.

"It's all so exciting," she told Anne, so moved she could barely speak. "The children growing up. It's a wonderful time." This was true. For years, the summers had blended into each other, each much like the last. But now every summer would bring new developments. Mimi, then Billy, starting college, getting married, having children of their own. Of course there was sadness, the depressing reality of aging. (Anne: *I feel like a shriveled old hag.*) But Paulette refused to feel as Anne did. She had been the pretty one in the family, a distinction she'd enjoyed her whole life. Now she would cede the title gracefully. Watching Mimi clear the table, she was proud of her own generosity.

Good for you, sweetheart, she thought. *It's your turn.*

Inside the house, the telephone rang, a shrill intrusion. There was nobody out in the world she wanted to talk to. Everyone she needed was right here, close enough to touch.

"Paulette," Martine called through the open window. "Frank's on the phone."

"Daddy!" Scott cried. "Let me talk to Daddy!"

"In a minute," she said, rising. "Let Mother talk to him first." She hurried into the kitchen. The house's only telephone, a rotary model heavy as a bowling ball, sat on the counter. "Frank?" She drained the wine from her glass. "Is everything all right?"

"Hi." He sounded rushed, agitated. "Listen, I only have a minute, but I wanted to tell you. I think I can get down there this weekend." She heard the clack of a typewriter. Frank was always doing two things at once.

"What are you typing?"

Mimi came into the kitchen then, loaded down with dishes. *Excuse me,* she mouthed. She placed the salad bowl in the sink.

"More revisions on the paper. Sorry. I need to get this thing out the door."

Mimi bent over to scrape the plates into the trash. Paulette stared at her suntanned legs. The denim shorts—she hadn't noticed, until then, quite how short they were—rode up dramatically, revealing the bottom crease of her buttocks. For a moment, Paulette saw the girl as Frank would see her. She felt her throat tighten.

"Are you still there?" Frank asked. "I'll try to make it down there on Friday. It won't be easy, but I think I can swing it."

No. Paulette felt again the wave of sickness she'd felt watching Mimi at the beach, sour and corrosive, sharp as glass. Her family, summer at the Cape, her love for this dear girl: these were precious things, and fragile. Too delicate to be placed in Frank's careless hands.

"Frank, I know you're busy. You don't have to come if it's too difficult. I shouldn't have pressured you."

"That's okay. I want to." He lowered his voice. "I'm not good at sleeping alone."

More typing, a bell sounding; he had reached the end of a line.

Endless days. The blond expanse of the National Seashore, the sand fine as sugar; coarse tails of sea grass undulating in the wind. The days were cut along a template. Each morning, sandwiches were made, a basket packed. Damp swimsuits were retrieved from the line. For the rest of her life Paulette would remember these summers: the quiet richness of those days, the life of her family unfolding like a flower, ripening as it was meant to, all things in their proper time.

One morning, the car loaded, she noticed a child missing. "Gwen!" she called. "Where's Gwen?"

"Back porch," Scotty said.

Paulette found her curled up on a chaise lounge on the back porch, still in her nightgown. Paulette hadn't seen her since breakfast. With three adults and five children in the house, Gwen had gotten lost in the shuffle.

"Gwen? Get dressed, darling. We're going to the beach."

"I'm not going." Her cheeks were red, her mouth set. Paulette had seen this look before, after an altercation with her brothers, an unfair reprimand. It was a look that meant trouble.

"Gwen, don't be silly. Everybody's waiting. Mimi, and Charlotte."

"I don't want to go."

"What's the matter?" She laid a hand on her daughter's forehead to check for to a fever, only half joking. Gwen was crazy for the beach. At the end of the day, shivering, sunburned, she clamored for an extra half hour. Paulette often resorted to blackmail—strawberry ice cream at the general store in town—to get her to leave.

Gwen shrugged away her mother's hand. "I hate the beach. It's no fun any more." She kept her eyes on the ground.

Paulette frowned. Gwen had a sunny disposition: more extroverted than Billy, who was prone to moody silences; less rambunctious than Scotty. She had always been the easy one.

"I hate Charlotte," she said vehemently. "She won't even go in the water."

"Well, you can swim with your brothers. And Aunt Martine."

"I hate my bathing suit," she said, her chin trembling.

Paulette sat next to her. "What happened? You liked it a week ago." They had shopped for the suit together, making a day of it, lunch and shopping at Filene's downtown. Charmed by the little ruffle, Gwen had chosen the suit herself.

"I hate the stupid ruffle," she said now. "I look like a big baby."

"Sweetheart." Paulette chose her words carefully. She'd known this conversation was coming; she just hadn't imagined it would come so soon. "Are you upset because Charlotte looks so different all of a sudden?"

Gwen would not answer.

"It's strange for you," she said gently. "To see Charlotte growing up."

"But I'm *older*. Her birthday isn't until *December*." Gwen's face reddened. "It isn't fair."

"I know. It isn't." Paulette brushed the hair back from Gwen's forehead. "When I was your age, I was the smallest girl in my class. I came back to school in the fall and it seemed that all my friends were entirely different people. They were taller, and their figures were changing. And I hadn't changed at all. I was exactly the same."

Gwen stared up at her, her eyes rimmed with red.

"Back then they called it being a late bloomer. It took me a little longer, but it all happened eventually. And when it did I was very glad." Paulette drew her close and Gwen settled in. She was a cuddly child, more affectionate than her brothers. The difference, Paulette supposed, between boys and girls.

"I know what we can do. Let's get you a new bathing suit. A two-piece, like Charlotte's. We can drive into Provincetown tonight."

"Okay," Gwen said grudgingly.

Paulette stood and held out her hand. "Come on. Everybody's waiting." *Thank God that's over,* she thought.

For girls it was never simple. Later, riding in the car, shading her eyes against the morning glare, Paulette thought of her own puberty. All these years later, the memory still pained her: the interminable months of waiting, her failure so conspicuous, displayed for all to see. In her long sunny childhood she'd never felt envy, but at puberty it filled her every waking hour. She envied ceaselessly, obsessively, the few classmates who, heaven knew why, seemed to transform overnight. She'd hated them blindly, indiscriminately; hated even Marjorie Tuttle, her dear good friend. Now, as a mother, she remembered those girls with compassion, knowing they had faced their own difficulties: attention from older boys, grown men even; foolish adults like Frank who couldn't distinguish between a woman and a child. Once, twice, she'd caught him ogling girls barely out of grammar school. *I'm not a pervert,* he insisted when she brought this to his attention. *How am I supposed to know?* She had to admit, it was a fair question. The girls had adult-looking bodies, and dressed to show them: miniskirts, tight T-shirts, sometimes with nothing underneath. She'd been lucky—hadn't she?—to come of age in more modest times. She recalled how, at Wellesley, they'd worn raincoats over their whites as they crossed campus to the tennis court. Those rules had existed to keep girls safe and comfortable. And, it seemed to her, to make things more equitable. Proper clothing kept the buxom from feeling conspicuous; it preserved the vanity of the shapeless and the plump. How cruel to be a girl now, with no such safeguards in place. To be exposed to adult reactions no child was equipped to handle, the lust and ridicule and pity, the creeping shame.

God help Gwen, she thought. God help us all.

The ferry was crowded with people: the young in college sweat-shirts and denim cutoffs, showing suntanned legs; the old in windbreakers and clip-on sunglasses, comfortable shoes and Bermuda shorts. There were a few windblown men, like Frank McKotch, in business attire; but most wore chinos and golf shirts. They toted bicycles and fishing tackle, suitcases, duffel bags. A group of longhairs carried tents in backpacks. The whole crowd inhaled the ferry smell—a potent blend of fish and diesel—and shouted to be heard over the engines. On every face, in every voice, a palpable elation: *We're almost there! We're going to the Cape!*

Frank watched them in mute puzzlement. He witnessed the same phenomenon each summer in his wife and children, his decrepit in-laws. Even his sour sister-in-law displayed a brief burst of enthusiasm. The Drews considered Cape Cod their birthright. Summer after godblessed summer, they did not tire of strolling its beaches, sailing its shores, guzzling its chowder. For heaven's sake, what else was summer *for?*

He could think of a hundred answers to this question, or a thousand. To him the Cape meant crowds and traffic, glacial waters, unreliable weather that often as not left you marooned indoors with a crew of whiny, disappointed children and restless, irritable adults. What, exactly, was the attraction? For once, he was stumped.

It was a sensation he had seldom felt. Frank read widely in all the sciences, in English and in German; he followed the latest developments in theoretical physics, the emerging field of string theory, with rapt interest. He believed, fundamentally, that all things were knowable, that the world could be understood. But when it came to the Cape, he simply *didn't get it.* Summer after summer, he landed at Provincetown with the same deflated feeling: *Okay, now what?*

He supposed it came down to upbringing. Didn't everything? His wife had spent half her childhood on the water, or near it. She could swim, sail, dive like a porpoise. Frank was twenty before he caught his first glimpse of the ocean, on a road trip to Atlantic City with some buddies from Penn State. His recollections were vague, clouded by alcohol: White Castle hamburgers, girls in bathing suits, cans of beer smuggled onto the beach.

The ocean wasn't the point, Paulette reminded him each summer. What mattered was getting The Family together. But Frank had never gotten too excited about anybody's relatives, his own included. Since his marriage, he'd made exactly three trips back to the Pennsylvania town where his father still lived. The place paralyzed him with sadness. The company houses, the black smoke of the steel mills. His mother had died early and horribly, a metastatic breast cancer. Grief had turned his father stern and silent, or perhaps that was simply his nature. A dour old man, fatalistically pious, plodding through the years in mute patience, waiting for his life to be over. Frank couldn't imagine him any other way.

The family Frank had married into seemed glamorous by comparison. They had attended the best schools, traveled widely; in youth they'd been cherished and guided and subsidized in ways Frank had not. He didn't resent these distinctions. On the contrary: he wanted to be absorbed by the Drews, to become like them. He was prepared to love Roy and Martine, old Everett and Mamie, the army of blue-eyed cousins converging in Truro every summer (Drew cousins only: no one invited or even spoke of Mamie's tribe, the ragtag Broussards). But Frank—from a part of the world where people pronounced their Rs—wasn't a Drew and never would be; if he'd had any illusions on that score, they'd been shattered long ago. Now Frank counted himself lucky to be free of the family neuroses, which seemed congenital: Paulette's prudery, Martine's bitterness, Roy's laziness and self-importance; their unconscious sense of entitlement and absurd reverence for the Drew name, which no longer meant a thing to the rest of the world, if it ever had. To Frank, who was smarter and more industrious, who'd busted his ass for every break he'd ever gotten, the success of a guy like Roy Drew was insulting.

The horn sounded. Dieseling loudly, the boat approached the dock. Frank rose and waited; there was no sense in fighting the disorderly mass of humanity scrambling to disembark. Finally, he stepped onto the gangplank and spotted Paulette waving from the crowd.

"Frank! Over here!" She wore a navy blue dress that fit close at her waist. Her bare arms were white as milk. Several heads turned to look at her. This happened often, and still excited him. *My wife,* he thought proudly. *My wife.*

"Hi," he said, scooping her into his arms. She smelled of the outdoors, sea air and Coppertone. "Where are the offspring?"

"I told Martine we'd meet them. She took them to the beach."

"I have a better idea." Frank kissed her long on the mouth. "Let's go somewhere."

"Don't be silly." She stepped back, smoothing the dress over her hips. "Everybody's waiting for us. Scotty's out of his mind. Daddy, Daddy. It's all I've been hearing for days."

She handed him the keys to the wagon. Frank always drove when they were together; he hadn't been her passenger in years, not since the hair-raising spring when he taught her to drive. It was an arrangement they both preferred. Sitting in the passenger seat, he made Paulette nervous, and the feeling was mutual. Her style was to roar down the highway like an ambulance driver, slamming on the brakes at every yellow light. Two years before, to his horror, she had totaled his brand-new Saab 97, a car Frank loved in a way he would never love another. He forgave her immediately, grateful she wasn't hurt; but the car's demise still haunted him. He would drive it occasionally for the rest of his life, in dreams.

On the road to Truro she filled him in on the week's events. Martine had taken the children fishing; next week, winds permitting, Roy had promised a sail to Nantucket in the *Mamie Broussard*. There had been a few squabbles between Charlotte and Scotty, who'd been even more rambunctious than he was at home. It was a complaint Frank was tired of hearing. *What do you expect?* he wanted to say. *For God's sake, he's a boy.*

"What about his diet?" he asked instead. "Are you watching his sugar intake?"

They turned down the dusty lane that led to the Captain's House—an outstanding example of shingle-style architecture and, in Frank's mind, a monument to the financial ineptitude of his father-in-law. A century ago, the Drews had been one of the wealthiest families in America, thanks to one ancestor who'd amassed a whaling fortune. The old captain had helped build the railroad from Taunton to Providence and had owned property—acreage on Martha's Vineyard, a grand house on Beacon Hill—that was now worth millions. A small fortune for each of them, if his descendants had simply hung on to it; but Paulette's father, born into money, seemed constitutionally unable to earn any himself. Everett Drew had sold off the family assets one by one, pissing away the proceeds with a series of disastrous investments. Now that Ev had retired to Florida, his law firm was in the hands of Paulette's brother Roy, a guy less principled than his father and, in Frank's opinion, even less competent. The house in Truro was the last significant Drew asset. Within a few years, Frank imagined, it would slip through Roy's fingers.

They got out of the car and climbed the stairs to the front porch, where Roy Drew sat smoking a cigarette. He was a tall, spindly fellow with a receding hairline and a long, aquiline nose. An aristocratic nose, Frank thought, suitable for looking down.

"Roy! You made it." Paulette embraced her brother. "We were starting to worry."

Roy offered Frank his hand. "You had the right idea taking the ferry, my friend. Traffic was murder. Welcome."

Frank smiled grimly. The *welcome* rankled. It was Roy's way of reminding him who would inherit the house in a few years. Paulette had always been her father's favorite, but Roy was the son—and in the Drew family, tradition always trumped sentiment. Already Roy had benefited unfairly, making partner in the firm at the puppyish age of thirty. Since Ev's retirement, Roy had handled his parents' finances; their assets, Frank imagined, were being siphoned off at a discreet rate into Roy's personal bank account, to cover the new Mercedes, the endless maintenance on his boat. By the time the old man finally died, his will wouldn't much matter. Roy would already have socked away most of the take.

Roy offered him a cigarette. "No thanks," said Frank. *Better cut back on those things,* he thought. *Hang around long enough to enjoy my wife's inheritance.*

"How's the lawyering?" he asked briskly.

"What can I say? We're having a great year." Roy leaned back in his chair, stretching out his hairy legs. He wore runner's shorts, cut to the upper thigh. Nothing uglier than a man's legs, Frank thought.

"Glad to hear it," he said, clapping Roy's shoulder. "Good for you." His duty done, he followed Paulette into the kitchen, where Roy's skeletal wife was packing a picnic basket. "Hi, Anne," he said, kissing her cheek. Like her husband, she reeked of cigarette smoke. "Where are the kids?"

"Martine took them to the beach." Anne had wrapped half a dozen sandwiches in waxed paper. "I'm heading there right now."

"Where's Mimi?" Paulette asked.

"Oh, she met up with a girlfriend from school. Her parents have a place on the Vineyard." Anne returned the cold cuts to the fridge.

"Oh, that's too bad." Paulette turned to Frank, beaming. "Mimi is growing into a delightful young woman. I'm sorry you missed her."

"Me too," Frank said, though he hadn't seen Roy's kids in years and in truth, had never been able to keep their names straight. He thought of the empty house, the quiet front bedroom: a rare opportunity to get his wife alone at the Cape.

"I'll go get my bathing suit," Paulette said.

Frank watched her climb the stairs. "We'll meet you over there," he told Anne. "No sense waiting around for us."

At the bedroom door he waited a moment. Hard years of marriage had taught him that timing was key. If he waited until she'd undressed, a yes was much more likely. He opened the door.

"Frank!" Paulette stood in the center of the room, naked as a newborn. She was about to step into her swimsuit. "Someone could be in the hallway. You really should knock."

"Nobody's there." He went to her and pulled her close, before she could cover herself. He felt the tension in her shoulders: a no was still possible.

"Anne and Roy are waiting downstairs."

"Don't worry. I said we'd meet them over there."

She relaxed in his arms then, the signal he'd been waiting for. "I did miss you," she said in a small voice, as though it were an admission of guilt.

"Let me look at you." They always made love in the dark; it was a rare thing to see her naked in daylight: her tiny nipples, the lush dark hair.

He laid her down on the bed, a little roughly. "I thought about this all week."

Frank followed his wife an endless mile up the beach, loaded down with an Igloo cooler, an umbrella and two beach chairs. His feet sank into the soft sand. Tomorrow morning—he knew this from experience—he'd have a powerful backache.

"How about here?" he suggested, dropping the cooler in the sand.

Paulette shaded her eyes. "No. Over there." She pointed to a pink umbrella far in the distance. Like all the Drews, she had firm convictions about what constituted a suitable location for lounging on the beach. She'd make him trudge through the hot sand for fifteen or twenty minutes, then choose a spot that, to Frank's eye, was indistinguishable from any other.

They trudged onward. Sweat dripped down Frank's forehead and into his eyes. A small plane buzzed overhead, trailing a lettered banner: SULLY'S CLAM SHACK BEST CHOWDA ON THE CAPE.

"Here," Paulette said finally. "This is perfect."

Frank spiked the umbrella viciously into the sand. He despised the beach. The sun was unkind to his freckled skin; while the Drews basked, he reddened, perspired, longed for a drink. *Bring a book,* Paulette suggested. *Take a nap.* But reading in the sun made his head ache, and Frank hadn't napped since he was in diapers. Instead he sat for hours doing nothing. The inactivity caused him almost physical anguish. Why Paulette insisted on torturing him this way—what satisfaction she got out of keeping him trapped, idle and bored out of his mind—he would never understand.

He opened the beach chairs and settled them under the umbrella. His objections went beyond boredom. It was the ocean itself he hated, its droning eternality. *It puts everything in perspective,* Paulette sometimes said, and that was Frank's point precisely. He didn't want to be reminded of his own insignificance, the brevity of his life, the pettiness of his concerns. What kind of lunatic wanted to think about that?

He stretched out under the umbrella and shaded his eyes from the sun. "Hey there!" a familiar voice called. "We're over here."

His sister-in-law Martine jogged toward them, her compact body fit and sexless in a no-nonsense blue suit. Frank rose to greet her. He couldn't think of another woman whose near-nakedness affected him so little.

Paulette sat up on the blanket and waved to Scotty and Gwen, wet and blue-lipped under a striped umbrella, wrapped in beach towels. She shaded her eyes. "Where's Billy?"

"He rode into Provincetown on his bike," said Martine. "That's okay, right?"

Paulette frowned. "There's a quite a bit of traffic on that highway. Frank, do you think he'll be all right?"

"Don't be silly. The kid can handle himself."

"Daddy!" Gwen called, running toward him. Another, taller girl followed behind.

"Hi baby!" he called. "How's the water?"

"Cold!" She grasped him around the waist. Her head was wet against his shirt front. "Do you like my new bathing suit?"

"I love it." He scooped her into his arms. On her, the purple bikini was adorable, the top placed roughly where breasts would be. Half of it had gone slightly askew, revealing one pink nipple. He tugged it gingerly back into place.

"Darling, you're burning." Paulette reached into her bag for a tube of zinc oxide. "Put this on your nose."

"I could use some of that too," said Frank. The poor kid had inherited his complexion. He took the tube from Paulette's hand, put a dab on his own nose and rubbed it onto Gwen's. She giggled, delighted.

"Hi, Uncle Frank," said the other girl, who had joined them.

"Hi there." Frank bent to kiss her cheek. "I thought you went to the Vineyard."

"That was Mimi," said the girl. "And her stupid friend."

"Oh, *Charlotte.*" The younger one, then; she was Gwen's age. He eyed the two standing side by side. Like Gwen, Charlotte wore a bikini, but she had small breasts to fill hers. Her shoulder was level with the top of Gwen's head.

"I'm freezing," said Gwen, her teeth chattering. "Daddy, we're going to lie down on our towel."

He watched them climb the dune, Gwen's sturdy legs pumping. "That's Charlotte?" he said to his wife, whose nose was buried in Willa Cather.

"Mm hm."

"She's twelve? Like Gwen?"

"Charlotte's three months younger. She'll be thirteen in December." Paulette turned a page.

The wind shifted, a sudden chill. Frank knew, could never again unknow, that something was terribly wrong.

Traffic was brisk on the road to Provincetown. Billy rode carefully, keeping an eye on his rearview mirror. He was a responsible cyclist; he kept to the right and always signaled before he turned. Most drivers gave him wide berth, but there was the occasional hoser who roared up behind him and leaned on the horn or flashed the lights. He was beginning to understand that life was full of such people—the aggressive, the crude. Once in awhile they paid for their bad behavior, but usually not. Mostly they took over companies, dominated sport teams, ran for president. Hosers basically owned the world.

It was the kind of thing his aunt Martine was always saying. *No good deed goes unpunished.* And: *The freaks shall inherit the earth.* He'd begun to see that it was true. The past soccer season had kicked the crap out of him. Coach Dick—his actual name—had humiliated him practice after practice. *He had a losing season, and you're his scapegoat,* Billy's father had told him, rather unhelpfully. *Never be a scapegoat.*

How do I do that? Billy demanded.

You'll figure it out, his father said.

Billy hadn't figured it out. He had waited it out. As of June first, Pilgrims Country Day was officially behind him. In the fall, he would go to boarding school in Maine, where the coaches would not be hosers. He'd been promised this by his uncle Roy, who had gone to Pearse a hundred years ago and probably didn't know what he was talking about.

Billy turned off the highway and down the beach road, heading for Provincetown. He'd know the right road when he saw it. Last night they had gone into town together, Billy, his mother and Gwen. Scotty hadn't been allowed to come because, according to their mother, he'd behaved abominably all day. As far as Billy could tell, that meant picking at his dinner, making rude noises at the table and teasing Charlotte who, in Billy's opinion, deserved it. Charlotte had turned into a giant pain in the ass. He felt sorry for Scotty, but was glad to be away from him. This year Scotty had the top bunk, where he snored and thrashed and talked in his sleep, waking Billy ten times a night. Billy hated sharing a bedroom. And his brother was only nine, a little kid.

In Provincetown, they'd had ice cream, Billy a chocolate cone with jimmies, Gwen a strawberry frappe. Then their mother led them into a shop called Outer Limits. In the windows were beach towels, T-shirts, bathing suits. A tie-dyed hammock hung from the ceiling.

We'll be a few minutes, his mother had told him. *You can look around. Just don't leave the store.*

Billy had walked around the shop. At the cash register, under glass, was an assortment of strange pipes, one of which cost twenty dollars. There were earrings, shell necklaces, rings that changed color depending on your mood. In the back, he found racks of postcards. The National Seashore, the Provincetown lighthouse, whales, lobsters, girls in bikinis. An entire rack was devoted to pictures of men in uniform: policeman, fireman, soldier in camouflage. Billy took one of the cards and slipped it into his pocket.

He had stolen for a long time. Little things only—comic books, pocket knives, things he didn't really want. At the drugstore in Concord, he'd stolen four tubes of Crazy Glue. Why, he didn't exactly know.

He looked over his shoulder. To his horror, a clerk was coming toward him. He had never been caught before, and he wondered what the clerk would do. As always when he was nervous, he had an immediate urge to pee.

Hi, said the clerk. He reminded Billy of a pirate. His head was wrapped in a blue bandanna. He wore a tiny hoop earring in his right ear.

What are you doing here? The clerk's tone was friendly, not at all menacing. He didn't see me, Billy thought, confused.

My sister is getting a bathing suit.

The clerk perched on the corner of a low display case. *Are you staying in P-Town?*

Our house is in Truro, Billy said.

The clerk nodded toward a bicycle leaning against the display window. *Is that your bike? Or did you drive?*

My mom drove us. I'm only fourteen.

Oh. The clerk stood, glancing over his shoulder. *I thought you were older.*

Is there a bathroom here? Billy asked.

Not for customers. There's a public one at the bottom of Commercial Street.

Okay. Billy glanced back at the changing rooms. *If a lady comes out, tell her I'll be right back.*

At the bottom of the street he found the bathroom, a low barrack with no windows, made of cement blocks. He found the men's entrance, remembering his mother's advice to touch nothing but himself.

The bathroom was dark and smelled terrible, bleach and dampness and other things he didn't want to think about. He had a read a great deal about microorganisms. The average toilet was home to billions of viruses, parasites, bacteria. To Billy, they were like the dastardly supervillains Batman fought on TV. He imagined them masked, in flashy costumes. Evil Salmonella. Shit-loving Escherichia, the dirtiest organism imaginable: the very definition of filth.

He stood at the urinal and did his business. Zipping up, he heard a noise coming from one of the stalls.

The door of the stall was trembling, as if something were banging against it. Billy looked down at the floor. There were two pairs of boots in the stall, standing toe to toe. The door continued to shudder. When it stopped, he turned and fled.

He told nobody what he had seen. Who was there to tell? His cousin Mimi was older and knew more than he did; but when he saw her back at the house, sneaking a cigarette on the porch, he found himself unable to speak. For one thing, what exactly had he seen?

He had an idea about it, or maybe it was just a feeling. He kept his feeling to himself.

Now Billy parked his bike outside the shop and went inside. He looked for the pirate clerk but found a different one on duty, a suntanned girl in a halter top. He locked his bike to a lamppost and went down the street to the restroom, which smelled even worse during the day. The doors of the stalls were all closed. A pair of feet was visible beneath one of the doors: a man sitting down, his trousers around his ankles.

Billy washed his hands.

The man came out of the stall. He was old and fat, wearing red pants. Billy stepped aside to let him use the sink. When the man left, Billy examined his face in the mirror, thinking how the clerk had thought him older. Sixteen, old enough to drive.

Again he washed his hands. He was drying them on his shirt when a man entered the restroom. He was wearing a policeman's blue uniform, and Billy thought of the postcard he had stolen from the store.

The man stood at the urinal and unzipped.

"What are you looking at?" he asked Billy.

"Nothing." In his nervousness, his voice had cracked. He felt his face warm.

The man finished peeing and gave himself a shake. "Aren't you a little young to be hanging around here?"

"I'm sixteen," Billy said, his heart racing.

The man gave him a hard look. "I could get you into a lot of trouble. Now get out of here before I change my mind."

It was bedtime before Frank could get his wife alone. By then he had eaten dinner with the children, coated his sunburned shoulders with Solarcaine and thrown a Frisbee to Scotty for what seemed an eternity. ("Tire him out," Paulette had instructed him. "For heaven's sake, Frank, the child *will not sleep*.") He had endured hours of his brother-in-law's conversation: sailing stories, fishing stories, tales of masculine adventure in which Roy Drew emerged, always, as the hero. Frank knocked back four gin and tonics and moved his chair periodically, to stay upwind of Roy's cigarette smoke. Finally, he excused himself and climbed the stairs to Fanny's Room. Paulette was in her nightgown. She had just turned back the coverlet and was climbing into bed.

"There you are," he said.

"I was taking a bath." She gave him a wary look. *Once a day is plenty*, it seemed to say. *Don't think for a moment it's going to happen again.*

"I need to talk to you."

Her whole body relaxed, as though she'd been spared a punishment. Frank tried not to notice her relief. She listened closely as he spoke. Then, to his astonishment, simply shrugged.

"Oh, Frank. You know she's always been small for her age."

"It's more than that. Haven't you noticed? Seeing her with Roy's girl, I couldn't believe it. I can't believe they're the same age."

"All Gwen's school friends are taller than she is." Paulette said this lightly; maybe she meant nothing by it. Maybe it was who Frank supplied the subtext. *You would have noticed that if you were a better father. If you were ever at home.*

"Well, doesn't that concern you?" he demanded.

"Not at all." She smiled tightly. "I was the same way, at her age. I'm still petite. Like my mother, and Martine. All the women in my family are small."

"Of course," he said. "But she's almost thirteen. Shouldn't she be starting puberty by now? Breast development, pubic hair. Something."

"*Can you please lower your voice?*" Paulette's cheeks were scarlet, her voice a heated whisper. "Frank, I know a bit more about this than you do. I was a girl once. And it just so happens that I developed on the late side." She smiled grimly. "Maybe she'll end up like me. Wouldn't that be terrible?"

"What is that supposed to mean?"

"Let's not pretend." That smile again. "You prefer voluptuous women. I know that. I've always known that. But that doesn't mean there's anything wrong with the rest of us. Some men actually appreciate a slim figure. For heaven's sake, it's not a medical condition."

"Jesus, what's the matter with you?" He stared at her, dumbfounded. "I prefer *you*. I married you, didn't I?" As he said it, he knew it was hopeless. Hopeless to say he loved her, wanted her, had chosen her over numberless other girls. Hopeless to point out that *she* was the one who always said no, who regularly pushed him away.

He took a deep breath. "Listen. We're not talking about you. We're talking about Gwen. Something could be wrong. Medically, I mean." He waited a moment for this to sink in. "I think she should see a doctor. Just a checkup, to make sure everything is okay."

"She goes to the doctor. I take her every year. I've been taking her since she was a baby." Paulette's voice was perfectly even, a trick of hers: the further she pushed him, the calmer she became. "And Billy. And Scott. Frank, they are *perfectly healthy children.* And I am a good mother." She paused. "Lately, as it turns out, I am even a fairly good father."

"What is that supposed to mean?"

"Really, Frank. How many mothers have to teach their sons to shave?"

He colored. A few months back, Billy had found one of Frank's razors and cut himself, trying to remove the peach fuzz from his upper lip. Frank was out of town—the annual meeting at Cold Spring Harbor—and it was Paulette who'd helped the kid, something Frank would not be allowed to forget.

"You know, I find this really interesting." She seemed to be waiting for a response.

"What?" he said wearily.

"It's interesting that only time you've ever shown the slightest interest in our children's health, it concerns something sexual." She said the last word in a hoarse whisper. It would have been comical, he thought, if it weren't so sad.

"Sexual? Who mentioned anything sexual?" *I could kill this woman,* he thought. He felt his heart accelerating, his arms and legs flooding with blood. *No: she will kill me. She is subtracting years from my life.*

"Come on, Frank. You've always been obsessed with sex."

It impressed him that she pronounced the word at a normal volume. He knew his wife, knew the effort that must have cost.

Exercising heroic self-control, he did not answer. He'd been taught never to hit a girl, and that applied also to the verbal. He didn't say what he'd been thinking on and off for years: *You are the most repressed woman I've known in all my life.*

The night is still, and the house sleeps fitfully. In the front bedroom, the couple lie close together on the narrow bed. Each resents the other body, its warm breathing, its radiant heat. The man longs to slip outdoors for a walk, but fears waking his sister-in-law, an ill-tempered sentry at the top of the stairs. His wife feigns sleep, perspires into her cotton nightgown. She is too angry to sleep unclothed.

Downstairs, in the deep part of the house, their younger son is snoring. He dreams of the surf, the flying Frisbee, the dog they will not let him have.

His older brother lies awake in the top bunk, remembering boots in a bathroom stall: worn cowboy boots with intricate stitching, the others black leather, shiny and new.

On the screened porch the girl cousins sleep the deep sleep of children. A cool breeze kisses their cheeks.

In a year the house will be sold. Frank and Paulette McKotch will communicate through lawyers. It is the last summer for this family. Nothing will ever be the same.

Oakland

The street went up a slight rise and then angled up
toward the left, like a raised arm. There were four utility
poles on one side: each pole was a T with two crosses,
with the wires coming from each pole and extending
out in a messy radiance of black lines to the houses
and buildings of the street. The wires illustrated how
everything on the street was connected in this one way:
a web of electricity flowed through all the structures
like blood. On a gray day, you looked up to the electric
wires like the spines of an umbrella, on blue days
you forgot them because what you noticed were the trees'
green over you, and the blue past that green. Our house
was on the right side, middle of the block. In the first
half of our life in it, it was a cream-colored house
with blue and red trim. Later, we had it painted a light
olive and a dark green, the colors of river stones.
The yards used to be a jungle, but at some point we spent
a summer hauling things out and planting. A pergola
which the potato vines took over: a continuous mass
of little white flowers. Lavender bushes in a long row
on one side of the house, roses in a long row on one edge
of the side yard. The roses had always been there,
the cleaned yards now showed them to good advantage.
At the back: the apple-pear tree with black arthritic
branches, the sour tangerine tree beside it, and beside that,
the holly tree with pricking leaves. On the patio
was an old claw-foot tub converted into a flowerbed:
dwarf agapanthus, more lavender, daisies that never took.
Directly across the street, the house that I still think of
as Paul's, though he's been dead at least five years.
I had seen them take his body out, unceremoniously,
in the middle of the day, on a gurney. His daughter
and her family live there now. A few years before that,

his wife had died, a heart attack while in the shower.
This would be the very first death. And before our house,
built sometime in the 1920s, and before all the other
houses on the street and in the neighborhood, what
houses stood? Few enough houses, anyway, so that you
could see the way down to Lake Merritt. But our house.
The very house. Our house that is now as *madeleine*
to the larger mind of the place, and to my mind also.

To the Unborn

We have smoked all the cigarettes
and sold the last pack years ago
but I think you'll thank us once you read
the research—that much
we took upon ourselves. So,
remember: smoking kills. Beware
of radiation, mercury and ground-level ozone,
and for God's sakes, wear your seatbelts
in whatever kind of wacky cars you make.
We've left some ideas for those,
by the way. What else? Enjoy
the place—we wish it could have been
better, but we had long
retirements, most of us, and you know
how expensive *that* can be. How time
flies! I must admit, we were
caught off guard by some things. We hope
you get along, but if you don't,
there are plenty of nuclear weapons
for you to use—just keep in mind,
they really should be launched by
democratic nations, otherwise
all hell could break loose. Sorry
about the farmland, but at least there's a copy
of the latest food pyramid lying around
somewhere. So eat healthy!
And remember to take life one day at a time.
Lord knows it gets by quickly. The secret
of our happiness, I'd say,
was in accepting what we could not change.

PAULA BOHINCE

Cleaning My Father's House

I've come home, to sit inside this house
among the locusts and the crickets, their goodbye duet,
their chitter and squeak of *So long.*
Packing his things to make room for my own:
his pale blue Easter suit, his Bowie knife, its leather sheath
branded with *Nashville.* Catholic medals,
a finger's length statue of Christ in agony on the cross.
I touch the open mouth and put Him away.
So much stuff engraved upon a life. His wallet,
like a miniature and battered suitcase, still feels warm.
How can that be? Social Security card
soft as dishcloth, his license, expired now, a laminated
girlie picture behind it—blond barrel curls,
angora sweater unbuttoned.
I find the flannel shirts I gave him one Christmas,
press them to my lips, hungry for his scent of gasoline
and tobacco, pomade and Ivory soap.
Beneath the bed, slippery piles of Stagger Lee and Lena
Horne records, a dozen half-carved
wooden animals. Biographies of Custer, Billy the Kid.
I think my father was a boy, an unhappy child
who played with guns and trouble, who had a daughter
by accident, each of us bewildered by the other.
It's dark outside, end of the longest summer.
We met once, in this life. Even the ash in his ashtray
seems precious, impossible to be rid of.

Poem of Nine A.M.

Sing for us whose troubles

are troubles we're lucky to have:
cold orange juice, and cold coffee,

corridor after corridor, as our
circadian rhythms fall into place:

work is a refuge from home, and home from work.
We have task force reports,

but no tasks, and no force,
so far removed from concrete and crisp air

we might be living anywhere,
enjoying each other's company, within bounds.

    *

When I flew over the Grand Canyon, I loved—
who wouldn't?—to see the majestic gash in earth,

but what *moved* me
were the flat hints of grids

that began and ended several miles away,
tan, ecru, beige, knife-scratches on dry toast,

and then houses—some might have been trailers—so faint

and isolated next to those faint lines.
Single grains of sugar. Sesame seeds.

We should never look down
on what gives strangers comfort,

on what we learn too late that we might need.

An Explanation of Dark Matter

Nicole has this one friend
whose hand can burn straight through her clothes
& through the skin of her back. Like this,
she said, placing her hand on my winter coat,
the train above the East River, stalled.

Like this, the canary blossoms of Chinese witch hazel
flame into this world as astronomers believe dark matter does:
as evidence of an alternate reality, the gravity
of things there: a truck, a vase, a horse, a tea-kettle.

      *

Beneath the video clip of the soldier in a house in Fallujah
the caption translates his barely audible cry just before
he fires into the body of a man slouched against the wall:
"He's fucking pretending to be dead! He's pretending to be
    fucking dead!"

      *

But I think witch hazel
isn't fooling anyone; it is winter
& you must see the boiling yellow flames
as the pull & blossoming of this world.

We take a long shower this morning.
You ask if I heard, on the radio, what you thought you had
about the teenage girl trapped eight days in her car in a ravine
by the highway, found alive
after a neighbor saw her there, as the radio put it, in a very vivid
    dream.

Temporary Tattoo

Beside the cash register in my favorite used bookstore
I see a glass bowl of what seem to be postage stamps
until I look closer: temporary tattoos of red and green,

with ornate black lettering *Bruised Apple Books.*
Take one, says Andrew, *Take two,* as if he directs a film
about the struggle of an independent bookseller

and his aging clientele, some of them tattooed
in the Summer of Love, some of them tattooed
by surgery, or time. I take one

although I know a temporary tattoo
is oxymoronic, maybe just plain moronic,
something else the world does not need,

as no one needs the leather-bound collected Thackery
or the first-edition *Joy of Sex* inscribed *Love,*
from Guess Who? A tattoo should be permanent,

a commitment, a cross-hatched cobra coiled
around the biceps, inks of deep blue and green
like the veins that pop from the carney's arm

when he makes a fist. A tattoo should not
smear, dissolve with baby-oil-on-tissue,
should be bold as a snake swallowing a mouse

and the mouse-shape traveling the length of it
like a bad idea shaping a life, distorting a life.
The apple is pink-red, like the tip of a cigarette,

its single leaf the green of the 1964 Chevy convertible
on cinder blocks behind the bookstore,
a car that will never run

despite the young man who works
under the hood every night until dark.
Someone should go to him and tell him

the sum is not always greater than its parts.
Sometimes the parts are what is valuable,
what can be parlayed into a life.

Tell him sell the tires, sell the wheels.
Tell him there is not enough light in all of his days
to spend evenings with his back to the stars,

staining his hands with grease and oil.
Someone should give him the tattoo
of the bruised apple, which will last

a week, at best. Tell him the Chevy's time
has come and gone, that nothing lasts forever
except our desire for things to last forever.

But he is too young to know this,
and nothing can convince him this is true.
Nothing written in any of these books

can show him what his strong hands
seem to show as they fold the oily rag
and drop the hood on another day

and in the gravel lot behind the bookstore
the last of the sun shines
pink, and everywhere, and always.

Law of Return

Adler, Professor of Rabbinics (Emeritus), was annoyed that the young man sitting next to him was interfering with his sleep. Through slitted eyes he watched him, plugged into his music, list lessly turning the pages of a magazine, giving out somehow all the traits Adler had come to dislike in the young—vanity, narcissism, the insouciant attention of the dilettante. Adler audibly sighed and turned farther toward the wall of the plane, its cutout window, unyielding plastic eyelid drawn against the harsh California sun.

It had been a difficult several days, the conference long and stuffed tediously with talk, the antic chatter only academics could generate—a high school locker room, Adler often thought, just with better vocabulary. It seemed every second person was an assistant professor someplace, with a thesis Adler simply had to have a look at, maybe over lunch, an idea for a collaboration that simply couldn't wait. Stuck—feeling so literally much of the time, lumpily subsiding in chairs, feet heaving unwillingly when he walked—he had sat too long, drunk too much. Without Amelia there to warn him he had eaten all the food, the meats and thick sauces and whipped desserts, so that his bilious, enflamed innards mirrored his mood—or was it the other way round?—and he had exhausted himself politely trying to conceal both.

Finally in absolute misery he had called home last night. He had been sleeping, or hoping to—what little sleep he managed to snatch these days was fitful—when a dream came over him that he was being crushed to death. A weight, slowly growing, pressed on his chest until his breathing caught and he had not even the strength to cry out. He had opened his eyes, alone in a strange room, thrown aside his glasses and the book that had fallen under his chin without noticing either. Through the curtains dim city light revealed the television in its sleek black case, the staring white telephone, and draped over a chair his pants, the loose belt dangling—but only heightened their strangeness, as if he had never seen them before. Where had he come? Swallowing panic, he dialed the number, though it was four in the morning in New York, and waited in the darkness for Amelia to stir and answer.

She had, blessed woman, taken care of everything. What about his medicine? Yes, two spoons after dinner. He could have two more. Did he ask for the extra pillow so he wouldn't lie flat? He had forgotten. Was he reading when he went to sleep? With furtive pleasurable relief Adler located the book on the floor, the reading glasses beside it. Her voice was a balm, a warm soothing he could almost feel around the shoulders. She didn't even sound tired. "Darling," he sleepily told her. "Please. I have to come home."

She had booked him on an earlier flight—he would miss the conference's final day, the banquet where he was to be honored, but nothing could have concerned Adler less—and though there was no room in first class, Amelia had secured the bulkhead for him, the side with only two seats, and thankfully the one next to Adler was free.

After a few hours of delightful sleep, blank, refreshing, Adler had risen twenty minutes before his wake-up call, showered, dressed, and left a brief friendly message for one of the conference organizers at the front desk—"Called back to New York, unavoidable. Much enjoyed. Regards to all, Adler". Packed and ready, he paused by the full-length mirror on the closet door to look at himself. This was not a pursuit of conceit. He had developed this habit as a young logician, saw it as an exercise in confronting each day the world as it plainly was, beginning with yourself. He neither delighted or shied away from what he saw this day, a rough-shaven, solid-looking man, seventy-five in two months but objectively could be mistaken for sixty-eight or nine, heavy eyebrows beneath a receded margin of hair, lips expressively full, eyes clear, undaunted—he stood, saw what he saw, and moved away. It was Adler's reasoning that life was there all the time looking at you, all you needed was the courage to look back.

At the airport he was one of the first to board. He joked with the stewardess, a pretty young woman with blonde hair falling attractively from a loose bun. Her nameplate, under a pair of silver wings, read Maureen, a name Adler happily associated with lively Irish actresses in movies from his youth. He put a hand on her arm and asked was the plane safe, and Maureen assured him with a confidential smile it was, she had checked it herself. She took his coat and placed in the bin, and Adler removed some papers and a book from his briefcase, was about to hand it to Maureen as well, then changed his mind. The briefcase, a present from Amelia and Shelly for his retirement, was Italian leather, deep maroon lovely to the touch, with his initials, SKA, embossed by the handle in gold. The combination to the latches was the date of their wedding anniversary, and Shelly had joked through surprising tears Adler had better not lock it, in case he ever need ed to get anything out. He smiled, remembering the elegant, candle-lit restaurant three months ago, the waiter wheeling in a draped white cart with the wrapped present and another bottle of champagne, his only child, so often, frankly, a disappointment, moved to tears. He rubbed a fingerprint from a clasp, yawned luxuriously, and decided he would keep it beside him. Propping the silly wafer of a pillow against the window, before the plane had even taxied from the gate, Adler was again deliciously asleep.

At the culmination of a distinguished career, Adler regarded his life as a long, often arduous journey from which he had emerged aged but triumphant. Eight books, some still read, nearly a hundred scholarly essays, member of a dozen societies and editorial boards. Honorary doctorates hung alongside his own pair in his study, with a medal from the Chancellor of the State University System of New York presented at his retirement. It was widely accepted that Adler had, single-handedly, turned his department from a flagging and obscure outpost into a nationally recognized center for Judaic study.

For years the girls—he enjoyed calling them this, his wife, his daughter—had been urging Adler to slow down, take things more easy. His own father was already dead ten years at Adler's age, swept off by an aneurysm in the brain. His mother, too, was gone, victim of a more agonizing disease that wasted her last years in misery. He should have needed no cautioning. Fear itself, not to mention common sense, might have made his choice clear. But to walk away from all he had built was difficult, especially now it was under threat. When Adler was coming up, in the old days, just teaching a class in Jewish history or ethics seemed a duty, the prideful obligation of every person who had been on the lucky side of the water during the war—to preserve an essence of Jewish life and sensibility before it frayed entirely and, as the doomsayers liked to say, handed Hitler the final victory in his grave. And Adler, energetic Rationalist, a free man in a free world, looking back not only to the sacred texts but embracing as well the Enlightenment, Spinoza and the Cartesians, had, it soon became apparent, also found a way to look forward.

The next generation he had taken in stride, the nervous and excitable intellectuals with their French demigods and impenetrable jargon. They respected him, seemed to think they spoke the same language, which suited Adler, who had no idea what they were talking about, just fine. But a new breed more recently appeared worried him, the assertively religious determined to yank the whole culture back to some *shtetl* fantasy, the sinkhole of threat and poverty and doom effaced for them in a blurry pious sentimentality that turned Adler's stomach. At a faculty meeting one of them, a brand new Assistant who quoted his own thesis, whose dim prospect of tenure, Adler privately thought, grew more and more unlikely every time he opened his whiny mouth, had the impudence to stand up and lecture them on the need for greater emphasis on *Yiddishkeit* in the classroom. This in a Judaic Studies Program. He stood, sallow, determined in his daily black suit, with the beard of an adolescent fanatic, two fingers unconsciously rubbing the fringes of the prayer shawl loosed from his jacket like a display of moral resolve the rest of them were too cowardly or corrupt to adopt. At his interview, Adler recalled, he had felt some distant sympathy, not for the labored if efficient work, certainly not for the air, mildly aggrieved even then, of martyred devotion, but for the nervousness, the shy attempts to impress, to test the waters of a new sea. Something— he irritatedly had no idea what—had reminded Adler of himself. After giving the boy plenty of rope to hang himself, Adler silenced him with one of the steady frowns he was famous for (this was a meeting to discuss the *budget,* he quietly admonished), and the chastened young professor, mumbling inaudibly (reciting *Psalms,* Adler uncharitably thought) resumed his seat. Adler turned his attention off like a light switch, swallowing visions of hauling him headfirst from the room by his nanny goat's beard.

So how could he leave? Then, six months ago, the decision was made for him. The ulcer had burst in January, surprisingly without pain, silently pooling his stomach with blood until one midnight he had staggered to the bathroom, almost too weak to get there, and what he saw when he stood up made him call out to Amelia. Two weeks in the hospital, transfusions too numerous to count, a needle in his arm every time he sneezed, the unspeakable humiliation of doing his business in a white plastic insert they had for him in the toilet, summoning a nurse to inspect the stinking evidence, while Adler turned away in bed wishing to die. Finally, bearing strict instructions about stress and diet, he was allowed to go home. When the girls again brought up retirement Adler, almost meekly, agreed.

They drove to Cape Cod where a realtor Shelly knew showed them houses. One, a converted barn on a half-acre overlooking a pond, they loved immediately, but Adler dismissed it as unthinkable. It would eat up every last nickel of their savings. To which Amelia said, Exactly, savings. What, exactly, have we been saving for?

And though Adler continued to fret, after the bonds had been cashed, the mutual funds emptied (they still had insurance, the university would take care of that, but what of a catastrophe, Adler worried. What about something entirely unforeseen?) Adler more and more envisioned himself in his new domain. A table on the upstairs porch, with its pond view and the trees beyond it. Amelia below, working in the garden, Shelly reading, maybe even—was it really too much to ask?—some grandchildren running on the lawn. Life's long work behind him, unchained from obligation and strife, his family gathered round. Slow summer afternoons with thick Russian novels, watching the sky change over the water.

Dreaming of flight—no plane, just Adler, skimming clouds, negotiating leisurely rolls, dipping low now and then for a closer look—he was disturbed by a commotion in the aisle, a young man opening compartments overhead. Apparently discovering no room in any, he turned with a fixed expression to the pretty stewardess, who took his coat and shoulder bag, let her wait while he extracted some magazines, then turned again to stand waiting above Adler. It took Adler a befuddled moment to realize what the boy wanted and remove the papers and book from the empty seat, because, still groggy from sleeping—he could feel a slack trail of saliva on his chin—he was staring behind the boy and the stewardess at Meisel, wondering if he was real.

There he stood as Maureen gathered the young man's belongings, laughable crushed hat lopsided, pens and pencils sprouting from the pocket of a suit which couldn't have been new ten years ago, staring nowhere through thick glasses, that gaze—prim, destitute, quietly appalled—that had driven Adler nearly mad at the conference. As Adler watched Meisel worked something in his mouth and swallowed, pushed a finger under a grimy shirt collar for a comfortable scratch. What was he doing here? And then Adler, of course, remembered. He busied himself collecting papers, taking out his pressed handkerchief to wipe his chin, facing the window—confused to see they hadn't taken off yet—all the while hoping the rumpled man in the aisle wouldn't turn and notice him.

But he did.

Through averted eyes Adler sensed the recognition, the minute torsion of the head as it withdrew in disdain, so that, like some creature mesmerized by what it most wishes to flee, he felt compelled to turn his own head and look. Meisel gave his imperious, grizzled chin a ratchet upwards before letting his expression relax, the eyes intimately drooping, the smallest of smiles pressing thin blue lips in a line. Taking his time, he looked away—Adler still could not—and made his way toward the back of the plane.

Adler aligned his papers, put them with the book in his lap. He intended to give the boy beside him a look, a quick nod, acknowledgment without invitation—he never could get accustomed to planes, the way they shoved you willy-nilly within inches of absolute strangers—but the boy was fastening silver headphones to his ears and opening a magazine, too busy to take any notice of Adler, who, when he leaned against the window hoping feebly for rest, heard the hissing sputter of music, the barest unintelligible sibilance of words, and found sleep impossible.

He looked like Chekhov, the young and beautiful Chekhov, which was a joke. Despairing of sleep Adler watched him from the side. The same coal-black hair combed with a flourish, the same lovely articulate face, distinguished profile, down to the immaculate goatee. All he needed were spectacles on a ribbon—this Antonich wore black wraparound sunglasses, even in the plane's near dusk—to be a dead ringer. What a joke. This kid wouldn't know Chekhov from Charlie Tuna, would think he was a spy or some athlete, one of those imported hockey players. Chekhov, whose tales of simple lives lived simply Adler (whose own blood lines ran to Russia, disappearing somewhere between Grodno and the Black Sea) liked to dream over late afternoons. Chekhov and this imp. What a laugh.

He got out his pen, wrestled the diabolical tray table from the armrest, organized the papers before him and determined to get to work. But unable to, his gaze drifted out the window, where full day lit the cloud cover and formations as big as mountains massed at the horizon. Then from somewhere behind him, unaccountably piercing the engine drone, a voice, pitched, querulous, unmistakable: "Listen, Missus, peanuts I can't do nothing with. You got maybe some hot tea?"

Adler screwed his eyes momentarily shut and wedged his backside deeper into the seat. He returned his attention to the boy beside him.

It seemed he was a reader, perhaps just learning how. Unable to stop himself, Adler watched with revulsion as the boy noisily flipped the pages of two magazines, apparently skipping the articles but gazing intently at the advertisements, then lifted a water bottle to his eyes—he was blind, no doubt, in those idiot glasses—to make out the small print there. No book, nothing for the mind. He held the bottle before his face as if it were ancient parchment. Next a wrapper from a candy bar, twice, it looked like, all the while bobbing in moronic assent to the headphones spattering in his ears. When Maureen reached their row with the drinks cart he passed Adler his glass of tomato juice without looking, without even turning his head.

Quietly outraged, despairing of an entire generation, none too pleased with his own which must have, in its failures of example and moral guidance, had a hand in producing this one, Adler gulped his juice and undid the pinching seatbelt. Not standing— of course—the boy swiveled sideways so Adler could clumsily squeeze by.

But he had forgotten about Meisel. There he sat, a few rows back, a scarecrow in a short sleeved shirt with wide pink and blue stripes, sipping loudly from a paper cup with the teabag tag dangling. His hat was off, a big satin yarmulke which might once have been white but was now motley crusted browns, doming his distended bony skull. Adler was repelled. Though he would never admit it in public he considered yarmulkes an ostentation, a showy flaunting of piety, which was, after all, a private affair between a man and his conscience. He felt a spike of pain in his abdomen as he saw Meisel had two seats to himself, his trampled hat and shabby jacket, a bursting ledger of notes, newspapers spread all around. He was eating a bagel and whatever was inside oozed fatly over his lips. Adler felt a sluicing in his bowels and tried to hurry by without looking, but Meisel was waiting for him. He wiped his glistening mouth with a huge napkin and followed Adler's progress up the aisle. He was doing something with his lips, they stretched and quivered and parted over gummy clotted teeth, and Adler urgently tried to pass without discovering what the man was about. However, though he moved as fast as he could, roughly bumping a woman's shoulder and not stopping to apologize, he could not reach the toilet before registering the unavoidable knowledge that the repugnant little man was, with not much effort to succeed, suppressing the urge to laugh.

In shame and consternation Adler balanced on the thin plastic seat, helplessly filling the tiny chamber with odors and sounds. Twice he thought he heard the door rattle, which only had the effect of sending another loose spasm through him. The second time he said, "Coming," and "Just a moment, please," but not loud enough, he expected, to be heard. His thoughts careened wildly, Adler, careening also, trying to evade them. That sauce on the meat last night, he knew he would pay for it. Near him at dinner some graduate student wetly sneezing into a handkerchief, and when the basket of rolls was passed, Adler ill with horror, watching him finger every one before choosing. And—why this?—some recurring unease from his retirement party, coming out of the restroom to see Shelly and Amelia holding hands, and it seemed they were upset, the younger still crying, Adler despairing to see it—man trouble, again, or maybe her dead-end job. He had said some things, his tongue loosed by champagne, meant kindly even if the delivery was a bit rough. But could he be blamed? Taking a scientific appraisal of his daughter—thirty-seven, fourteen years in the same hole-in-the-wall accounting firm in Queens, unmarried, of course, body thickening toward middle-age, thin hair, never lustrous enough to justify its length, still long and unappealingly girlish, her constant lament about loneliness and love's deceit—what he saw was what he saw. He waited, gave them a few minutes to finish up, then smiling politely came up to the table and joined them. He had meant to ask Amelia about it later that night but had forgotten. Now, warding off these useless annoying thoughts, Adler readied a wad of paper, breathed deeply and waited for his racked body to empty itself. Behind closed eyes he could not shake the image of Meisel outside the door, looking around with exaggerated pique, clattering the knob.

It was the second day of the conference, Adler's next to last. He was reading his essay on the Ethical Tradition in Jewish Thought, a talk he had presented a dozen times and enjoyed now mostly as performance, standing back to admire here and there a stylishly handled quote, a forceful turn of phrase. In the audience, nodding at some favorite moments, smiles, people taking notes. At ease, in pleasure, Adler leaned into the language, anticipating the section where he linked Buber to Maimonedes, a small maneuver he was particularly proud of. Where was that sentence he liked so much?

His attention was distracted by a fuss in the room, someone squeezing into the front rows—there were seats farther back—excusing himself, apologizing in a stage whisper, dropping papers and needing help in retrieving them—his first glimpse of Meisel. Annoyed, his rhythm thrown, Adler paused in his delivery and poured a glass of water—the imbecile had perfect timing. The Buber reference, just coming, only worked if you remembered the remark about Maimonedes a page or so back. It was in the language, the echo needed to be in your head. Now half the audience was watching this comedian, who, finally reaching the lone empty seat, pulled a legal-size pad noisily from his briefcase, selected a pen from the bouquet in his jacket pocket, and perched both on his lap. He smiled at Adler in a friendly way, as if inviting him, personally, to resume.

Adler drank the water, filled the glass again, replaced the pitcher on the dais and turned a mild amused look at a face he recognized in the front row—Fish from Harvard? Goldallen from Davis?—as if to indicate that these disturbances were tiresome, even slightly embarrassing, but unavoidable—what could you do but move on with grace? Fish, or was it that editor from Indiana, what was his name?, read Adler perfectly, smiled ruefully and shook his head. Looking everywhere except at the little man with the legal pad Adler decided not to go back to the Maimonedes reference. He would move forward, and if the point was lost it would be a pity, but they could read it, after all, in his book.

The ovation was loud and sustained—as loud, Adler couldn't help but notice, as had greeted any talk thus far, and certainly longer. A few people, two whole rows toward the left, rose to their feet. Adler smiled a bit wearily, arranged his notes, nodded at acquaintances, then, with open palms signaled, Enough, enough. They were here for the ideas, weren't they? He was simply glad to contribute. Leaning over the microphone to be heard, Adler asked if there were questions.

A few mild and interesting questions were offered up and Adler was relaxed, garrulous, at his best—this was the part he enjoyed most. He was fluent in response and even now, fifty years in the field, felt himself to be as widely read as anyone. He could cull citations effortlessly, from the Talmud to the *Times,* from Moses, as he sometimes liked to joke, to Moses Mendelssohn. He had just made a wry oblique reference to the President and his current troubles, which had them all laughing, when he saw, from the corner of his eye, the little man get to his feet.

Adler scanned the room for hands, but seeing none, acknowledged Meisel, as if he had just this moment noticed him. With a smile and raised eyebrows, showing both politeness and tolerant amusement, Adler invited the question.

"Professor," Meisel said, clearing his throat, adjusting his glasses, inclining over the row in front of him as if he could not be heard, which he certainly could be, and forcing two people seated there to crane sideways to give him room. "Thank you, Professor," Meisel said. "A very entertaining speech, I enjoyed it." Someone toward the back tittered.

Adler was up to the occasion. In a patient voice he said, "You're entirely welcome. I'm always pleased to be entertaining," and laughter rose again from the back of the room, several voices this time. "Do you have a question?"

"Yes," the little man continued. "Thanks, yes." He flipped pages in his pad, speaking as he did so, and Adler had to lean forward to hear what he said. He was comic, absurd, his hat, which he still wore, looked sat on, his clothing like it had been slept in for a week. His glasses, which he kept reaching to adjust, kept sliding anyway. Nothing to do but get it over with. "I'm sorry," Adler said from the dais. "I'm afraid I couldn't hear you."

"Apologies," Meisel said and smiled again. He reached up and scratched something near his collar. "I was checking some notes. I wonder, Professor," and he straightened and raised his voice, "if you're familiar with the work of Baruch Spinoza, a Jew from Amsterdam, though later he relinquished all ties with our people, for which even now it is hard to forgive."

He pronounced the name with a hard "z" and an accent, Spino-tza, and Adler suddenly felt the urge to laugh himself. "Spinoza," he said, improving the pronunciation. "Yes, I've heard the name."

Meisel was looking around, as if for the first time noticing all the people. Something changed in his face and he groped under his collar again. Adler could see him swallow. Remarkable, Adler thought. Where had this specimen come from?

"I wondered," Meisel continued, leaning forward again, holding the pad before him like a script, "because he didn't come up in your excellent talk, which I was honored to be in attendance."

"Yes," Adler said dryly. "Actually, he did." Time to end this. The little man now was preoccupied with the people around him, looking first at the man whose shoulder he leaned over, then at the woman beside him. He smiled a thin wavery smile, causing both to look away. Adler felt pity rise up, and an annoyed embarrassment; this was, finally, too excruciating to watch. "I believe you came in after I had begun, is that possible?" he said, stacking papers. "Perhaps you missed that part." He smiled amiably. "I'd be happy to furnish you a copy of the talk."

He bowed at Meisel, around the hall, suggesting it was time, and past time, luncheon awaited. He slid his reading glasses into a pocket to a smaller, valedictory ovation and was stepping off the dais when he saw Meisel still standing with the yellow pad, slapping a hand ineffectually against the paper, trying to join in the applause. He hadn't budged. This was a true character; Adler would have to remember the details for Amelia. He stopped and said, "Yes? Is there something else?"

The applause slackened abruptly and people, gathering briefcases and programs, paused to look. The quiet in the room grew, oddly suspended. Only Meisel didn't seem to notice.

"Yes, Professor, thanks," he said, again fumbling the pad. "My late arrival, I apologize. They told me the wrong bus, here I'm a visitor." He tried to rub his forehead but succeeded only in knocking his hat yet further off center. "The driver, very friendly, a local gentleman, discovered my mistake. He directed me quickly to a taxi, but too late, I am afraid, a little bit."

One of the organizers, dapper Grunfeld from UCLA, with the diamond ear-stud and shined cowboy boots, whose Marxist reading of Heschel yesterday morning had installed Adler in a surly headache that lasted all day, approached briskly from the side. On his face, the clipped unswerving grimace of a born administrator. He would clear this up, not to worry. He had a hand out toward Meisel, who gave an alarmed look. Now there would be a scene. At the last moment Grunfeld glanced at Adler, who shook his head firmly and opened a hand at his side. Leave him, Adler meant, sharply annoyed at Grunfeld, at them all, himself included, staring at this poor fellow as if he could possibly threaten anybody. Didn't they see what the man was? And Grunfeld seemed to get the message; he stopped short of taking hold of Meisel, but stood close by, poised for action.

The people left in the room, perhaps thirty, lingered with the half-abashed curiosity of onlookers at an arrest. Adler was suddenly sick of them all. He walked down the three steps and approached Meisel. "No matter," he said quietly. "You're here now."

Meisel turned on him a delighted smile, held it a moment or two longer than was comfortable, until Adler looked away. Up close he was even more disconcerting, skin waxy, eyes unevenly spaced, mouth stuffed with overlarge, yellowed teeth, nervous face trailing odd, half-formed expressions. His suit jacket held not one but several stains below the pocket where successive pens had leaked. He began rifling his pad. "Professor," he said, suddenly whispering. "I want to give you this." Papers, a napkin, fluttered to the ground. Adler saw Grunfeld scowling at them. "Here," Meisel said, declaiming again, raising his voice to be heard. He adjusted his hat and read from a soiled page covered in close writing. "'Only that thing is free which exists by the necessities of its own nature, and is determined in its actions by itself alone.'"

The room was entirely hushed. Nobody moved. Meisel looked around in modest triumph, tore the yellow paper from the pad and held it out to Adler, his unsettled face fawning, importunate, proud. "Professor," he said. "Baruch Spino*tza*."

Adler hadn't even been aware there was any trouble. He had eaten lunch—a consommé with too much something, garlic?, and a chicken dish he'd been a fool to try—and was sitting in the hotel lobby with some colleagues, absently wondering which of the afternoon presentations he might unobtrusively skip to sneak upstairs for a nap. Behind a potted palm, in the adjacent nest of easy chairs, a group of young academics was drinking beer from bottles, talking too loud. Through the spiky fronds Adler saw another join them, gesture at the bank of meeting rooms and laugh. Adler heard "that troll who bothered the old man" (here one of them glanced Adler's way), the words "Meisel" and "bloodbath". The door they were looking at swung open, revealing Grunfeld, moving fast. With visions of the luxurious bathrobe upstairs, the cool, freshly made bed, Adler was about to excuse himself when they all heard raised voices from behind the doors, the sound of something falling. Adler smiled all around at the small group, as if he had been listening, enjoying their conversation, and got up to leave. But there was Grunfeld, thin tie flapping, face engorged, cowboy boots chuffing the carpet. Adler hoped he was headed elsewhere, stood back to give him room, but then Grunfeld had him by the arm. "Sam," he said—Sam? Since when Sam? Adler thought in annoyance. Grunfeld pulled him behind the palm and whispered, his breath uncomfortably warm on Adler's ear. "Sam, we need your help. We've got a situation."

Adler could smell Grunfeld's lunch, or more precisely whatever sweet liquor he had had with it, and found the smell repellent, oddly foul. Before he could respond, could think of something to cover what he really wanted to say: he was tired, in fact his head ached with weariness; he didn't actually like this Grunfeld, with his intent, gleaming eyes, his designer clothing and fluid, incomprehensible speech; that Adler was invited here as a guest, wasn't he?, surely he had done his duty, whatever it was they would have to take care of it without him—before he could utter a word, Grunfeld had Adler by the elbow, and like a cripple, he was guided firmly toward the conference room doors.

Inside, by the back table with its litter of coffee cups and sagging danish, two of the conference organizers stood, side by side, rigid with anger. Before them on his knees, by an overturned chair, was Meisel, whose name Adler still didn't know, gathering a thick scatter of paper which had somehow fallen to the floor. He had both lips in his teeth, was chewing and humming tunelessly to himself as he scooped papers with both hands into a pile. He saw Adler and, abandoning the mess on the carpet, came rushing over.

"Professor," he said, holding out hands which extended a good six inches from his green jacket sleeves. "Thank you." He was out of breath, as if he'd been running. A blue vein like a twisted finger pulsed in his forehead. "Simcha Meisel," he said, taking both of Adler's hands. "Ph.D. Properly, we haven't been introduced." He turned burning eyes at the two organizers, one of whom looked away, while the other returned his look with open hostility. "I very much enjoyed our chat before. Extremely enjoyable. I was explaining to these gentlemen..."

Grunfeld, there again, interposed himself between the man and Adler, rescuing him, he no doubt assumed. "*We* were just explaining, Sam," he said, easing Meisel off; Adler could feel the damp hands relinquishing their hold, "about procedure. About papers solicited by invitation. About review boards. About," and he paused to look over at Meisel, "how things, in the real world, are done."

He squared his shoulders, the pompous fool, and Adler watched Meisel squirm behind his back, trying to be seen. His hat appeared over one shoulder, then the other. "Perhaps I was misinformed," Adler heard him say, the petulant whine gathering force. "I was led to believe this was a conference in Jewish scholarship." And he wrestled himself to Grunfeld's side, needing to take off his hat to do so, and for a moment Adler thought Grunfeld would grab him by the neck and throw him down. He glanced at the overturned chair, the spilled papers. "I am a published scholar," Meisel was saying. "I have several credentials, twenty years experience teaching our youth at all recognized levels. My work on Spinotza has been read by experts—I could give you names— who guarantee it is of the highest interest, specifically pertinent to your topic..." Here, with a look that shocked even Adler, Grunfeld relented and let the man through. "To the nature of your conference," Meisel went on, replacing his hat with two hands, "what you and I were discussing so pleasantly, before, Professor, after your enjoyable talk." He looked at Grunfeld a moment, took wet lips between his teeth again and began to chew.

One of the organizers, Adler didn't even try to remember his name, said, with brutally measured civility, "Dr. Meisel insists he will give his paper today, uninvited. To whom he will give it, and where, he does not know, but he insists—and he tells us you have given your approval to the plan."

Adler looked at them all, wondering if he were falling ill. Whatever was in that soup, or the chicken, what if it was tainted? Or maybe he had the flu. He was aware of his insides all of a sudden, a sour and unstable taste filled his mouth, his neck and eyes began to throb. Meisel, chewing his lips, stared at him, wolfish, greedy, despairing. He had begun to hum again. He was deranged, clearly in need of professional help, and the intimate glowing entreaty in his face made Adler dizzy to see. Grunfeld, a step or so back, was slowly flexing his wrists, unconsciously preening youth and vigor, just waiting for the chance to use them. The other two by the coffee table perhaps agitated Adler most of all, because in them he recognized himself over the past thirty years, their tweedy umbrage and self-regard, barely contained rage—they stood identically, one arm tucked beneath an elbow, a loose fist tapping their chins, martyrs to decorum.

Now Adler really did feel ill. His vision swarmed, something clutched in his abdomen. He must get upstairs, off his feet. Must get to a phone and call Amelia. He opened his mouth to talk, found he had no moisture to speak with.

"Professor," he finally got out, speaking to Meisel softly, softer even than he had intended. Adler could see his eyes, watery animated globes, his weak, stubborn smile, some desperate confederacy taking shape in his mind. "My friend," Adler said, and Meisel's eyes were instantly red-rimmed, swollen with emotion. He looked as if he would weep with pleasure. "You must listen to these gentlemen," Adler said, exhausted. "Really. What can I have to do with this?"

As if the muscles in it had been cut, Meisel's face slid downward, collapsed. "You see," Adler went on, "these gentlemen are in charge. I am a guest only, invited by them. And there are, as they say, procedures." The man's face was unnerving. Adler, wishing he could look away, felt himself growing lightheaded. "I'm certain your paper is of the highest interest," he continued. "Perhaps you could present it next year in..."

He broke off, not even intending to complete the sentence, mesmerized by the little man's gaze, but Grunfeld stepped in, thinking Adler had paused for information. "Chicago," Grunfeld announced peremptorily, as if this were the point he had been trying to make all along.

"Yes," Adler said. "Next year in Chicago." And now he really had to leave. He nodded weakly all around and was conscious, as he made his way to the door and through it, easing it shut behind him, though it was one of those doors that swung on some silent mechanism and needed no help from him, that while the organizers came with him, one speaking to him in aggrieved whispers, Grunfeld running on ahead to some new calamity, Meisel, alone in the room, by the upturned chair and his scattered papers, had not moved at all.

Clumsily, at first unable to work the lock, Adler slid the bolt and opened the restroom door. He had had to wait yet another moment once he stood up, the fever or the stomach upset or perhaps just sitting so long, causing him to drop both hands on the metal basin rim and stand there, breathing deeply. He did not look at the mirror. Easing past people waiting in the cramped aisle, he readied a look of apology, of commiseration—they were waiting, true, but clearly he had been in some distress or he would not have kept them so—their situations were, in fact, similar, part of a continuum, so to speak. He assumed they, at least someone, would understand and looked from one face to the next but people either turned aside to make room or stared stonily ahead, except for a woman who greeted his abashed grin—about to raise both hands before him, a gesture of mock contrition—with a look of such hostility, he looked nowhere but ahead himself, and made his way haltingly to his seat.

The young man seemed to be sleeping, though music still pounded from his yellow ear plugs and Adler, through the sunglasses, couldn't see his eyes. He was perfectly still, his legs relaxed before him, hands in his lap, and he did not notice Adler, or move to make any room. One of his magazines, some tattooed, half-naked athlete scowling from its cover, was in Adler's seat—did he think perhaps Adler had disappeared? Or maybe—Adler was feeling too weak to muster much annoyance—it had slipped off his lap as he dozed and landed there, no one's fault.

Adler stood another moment, not wishing to wake the boy but needing, of course, to regain his seat, when suddenly he realized his case was gone. He had been sleeping, expecting the plane to be in the air when he woke. When he had it was gone. The briefcase had been beside him and when he opened his eyes this boy was slamming things and Adler's papers were scattered on the seat and his briefcase was gone. Swelling with rage and panic Adler nearly grabbed the boy by the shoulder to ask him what he remembered, behind the boy, behind the stewardess, the one who had been so nice, had stood Meisel, that rootless expression drifting across his face, masking imperfectly—it was as clear in memory as if he were seeing it now—masking the half-crazed laughter that threatened to erupt from his lips. The deranged fool had taken it! How he expected to get away with it, how he expected Adler not to notice, not to deduce it was some childish spasm of revenge—that none of it made any sense only more strongly indicted the despicable thief, who saw the world arrayed in a conspiracy against him and here, suddenly, a chance to strike it a blow in return. How obvious. How pathetic and insufferable and obvious. Adler remembered the man's weepy eyes on him yesterday, remembered, now, Meisel alone in the hotel coffee shop this morning—he had been in too much of a hurry to notice then—a green duffel bag at his feet, drooping over a coffee cup—and wondered why he hadn't strangled him when he had the chance.

Discarding his earlier tact Adler took hold of the boy's shirt. "Yeah," the boy said, eyes still impossible to see, and moved sideways to make room.

"Pardon me," Adler said brusquely, in the tone he employed in the lecture hall, one which indicated he was to be attended immediately. The boy, his legs swiveled away from Adler, turned a slow head at him. "Yeah," he said again.

"My briefcase," Adler said, disconcerted by the twin reflections of himself he saw in the boy's plastic lenses. "When you came in, it was there"—he pointed at the young man's chest—"perhaps you saw..."

The boy was shaking his head. "No, man, I didn't," he said.

"You didn't see it? A leather briefcase, maroon with gold clasps?" The boy was no longer looking in his direction, still shaking his head. Adler swallowed rage. He would make this pipsqueak pay attention. "Behind you," he said in measured tones, "when you came in, when you were looking for space for your luggage..." The boy rubbed his temple as if he had a headache. "There was a little man in a green suit and a hat," Adler went on. "Right behind you. Did you see him, perhaps?"

"Look, dude, I told you. I didn't see your bag."

"We're not, at this moment, discussing the briefcase. There was a man directly behind you in line. You kept him waiting while you entertained us all with your little performance over the luggage compartment." Adler was aware his voice was rising, saw people in the surrounding rows looking at him, and realized, in a surge of energy, that he didn't care. He would, if he had to, grab him by the neck, get this brat to talk with him, to remember Meisel slipping the briefcase off the seat. He would get the captain, and with the boy's testimony, have Meisel arrested. "Once again," he said, aware of his locution, his cadence clipped and precise. "There was a man behind you in the line. You were looking for room for your luggage. There was none. I'm asking you once again—did you see this man?"

The boy looked ahead a moment, rubbed his head again, then turned back to Adler. He didn't say a word.

Not believing it as it happened, Adler shot out an arm and slapped the boy on the face. He did it again. He snatched the dark glasses, was about to snap them in two, throw them at him, when he felt a hand on his arm. The boy sat there, his naked eyes dully blue, too pale, somehow. He touched his jaw and looked in Adler's direction, unfocussed eyes staring a little to his left.

"Sir," a voice said. "Sir, please," and Adler turned to see Maureen, in her hands his briefcase. "I took it, sir, when this gentleman boarded. To stow up front. You were sleeping and I didn't like to disturb you." She held the briefcase toward Adler.

She was looking at him, and two couples in the row behind. The engine throb faltered a moment then resumed. Another stewardess came up beside him, stood there. He handed Maureen the boy's glasses, took the briefcase. "I see," he told her. "Yes, of course. I see." To the boy he said, "It seems I... A misunderstanding. It was gone and naturally I..." He extended a hand which the boy ignored. "I owe you an apology," Adler said.

"It's all right," Maureen said, brightly, helping the boy with the glasses. "No harm done. Let's find you another seat, shall we? Plenty of room."

And he let her guide him, holding the briefcase to his chest, dimly aware of how he looked, his hair disheveled, his tie pinching to the side. "Here we go," Maureen said, and he sat, still unable to put the briefcase down, only distantly embarrassed as she leaned over him to fasten the seat belt.

Across the aisle, as Adler knew he would be, was Meisel. Not glaring, not twisting a smirk of righteous insult, but sleeping. Deeply asleep, mouth open, hat off, head thrown backward, preposterous yarmulke slipping toward an eye, lips slack before the crowded teeth. Something oddly, then queasily familiar surfaced in the face, in the lips or bony head, and Adler had to look away. And he remembered, for no reason he could understand, the night of his retirement party, coming from the restroom to see Amelia and Shelly at their corner table, the younger woman crying, the older reaching a consoling hand, how he had paused before walking up, disconcerted, hurt—whose party was this?—a longstanding simmer of annoyance and impatience with his only child—was thirty-seven even a child any longer?—with Shelly's chronic, almost willful failure to fashion a reasonable life for herself. He had said things, yes, about all the men, about not asserting herself at work, about marriage and childbearing. One remark, after she had revealed to them tearfully yet another breakup, angrily asking who wants a drink from the public trough, he particularly regretted, and got up to excuse himself and gather his wild feelings. He stood stupidly around a corner until a waiter came up him and asked was anything wrong, then moved toward their table. When he reached them the tears were dry, the hands in their laps, dessert—Amelia had ordered him a fruit plate—waiting. And Adler sat there, pretending along with them, drawing them into conversation about public affairs, an article he hoped to write, feeling, on this celebration evening, increasingly aged and alone, watching his family with a misgiving he could not make himself understand.

Turning toward the window, Adler, hoping for sleep himself, realized it would be impossible. He thought of opening the briefcase and finding some work, a book to read. He thought of asking Maureen if there wasn't another empty seat somewhere. But he did nothing. With the briefcase in his lap he watched Meisel sleep for them both, his face, in repose, finally still, though one eye from time to time set up a disconcerting flutter. He had something to say to the man, he didn't know what, maybe something friendly, maybe something helpful, maybe even listen to his insufferable—yet Adler would suffer it—article. Adler didn't know. He let his gaze drift emptily through the porthole window at a far landscape of unbroken cloud, and thought of what he would say when the plane landed, when Meisel awoke, when those alarming eyes asked again. He didn't know. It was a long flight and Adler hoped maybe it would come to him.

Jazz Below the Water Line

Fifty-six years ago I picked up a musical instrument for the first time with intent to commit jazz. It was a trombone left behind by another kid at the jazz record store where we both hung out. (He'd been snatched by Selective Service for the Korean War. I'd 4-F'ed out.) I got a single lesson from a young bassist I knew: "Don't puff your cheeks out." With that I began a pursuit which has lasted until now.

I once sat in a hallway eating barbecue with Louis Armstrong, both of us in the lotus position. I asked him how King Oliver had sounded in 1923 Chicago. He rolled his trademark eyes: "Man! He was murder!" From the back room of a bespoke tailoring establishment where I worked, I once watched Duke Ellington being measured, and selecting cloth, for half a dozen suits. (Mac, the head fitter, said he had "exquisite taste in fabrics.") I would otherwise go unbathed in the reflected glare of fame or the paparazzi-flashes of celebrity.

Jazz is like the famous iceberg. At its very tip are names like those above, Bechet and Morton, Basie and Holiday, Hawkins and Young, Coltrane and Rollins, Evans and Flanagan. Then come the mere greats. Below the water-line is a world where journeymen and apprentices play their gigs at jazz clubs and bars run by pathological optimists, restaurants hiding in suburban strip malls, and a miscellany of weekend "jazz parties" or "festivals." Occasionally some high flyer with a grasp of entertainment deductibles will hire them for a private party, or a museum will fund a "jazz concert series." Money is scarce in this world, which is why even some of the truly accomplished need day gigs. (The princelings with steady gigs in studios don't count.) Even a detailed list of the kinds of work done in mid-career by superior jazz players to pay the rent probably wouldn't scare off more than a few of the hopefuls who still come up.

Well below the level of working musicians are once-a-month meetings of geriatric "jazz societies," where old men play at dixieland or feeble swing. Add a great many regular living-room "rehearsals" by groups which will never perform in public, and you have it. I call the whole underwater part of the iceberg "my jazz world." Without it my life would have been much poorer, and I probably richer.

Except when recorded, the music is ephemeral, which is an odd part of its charm. Few experiences are more truly existential than playing improvised music in front of strangers. (If they applaud, they seem, and occasionally become, friends.) Relics of those sounds may hang in your mind's ear a long time, but what keeps them there is remembering the people you played them with.

In high school I got to hear the Ellington Orchestra often, for whole evenings, at the Meadowbrook in Culver City, thanks to a buddy whose father was head bartender there. The same friend had an album of Dizzy Gillespie and the Coleman Hawkins single on which Thelonious Monk played his first solo, which I can still hear in my head. We listened to these over and over. Before that I had been smuggled in to hear the Nat King Cole Trio before Cole became a household word as a solo act. But only my friend's 1-A notice got me trying to play.

In 1951, confronting a deceptively simple instrument on which to play with other rank amateurs, I had the wits to take a couple of classes at the Westlake School of Music in Hollywood. I could have skipped one of them, but the other, Harmonic Ear Training, proved the most valuable forty-five hours of instruction I would ever get in any subject. Westlake was full of vets on the GI Bill—a pleasant madhouse, and the madness was bebop. The little practice cubicles vibrated day and night with horn players raising their notes-per-second rates. In class my teacher Dave Robertson would translate bulletins from the office like this: "If you hypes don't stop stashing your works in the toilet tanks, they will be confiscated."

Dave was a gnomish blond young man, a fine bebop pianist who didn't play gigs, or fraternize with students. He was there to teach our ears, and we spent our three hours singing back to him, bottom to top, the increasingly complex chords he would feed us, one at a time. He knew exactly how far along each of us was, and how to keep pushing us individually. To get our (or the government's) money's worth we sang back one another's chords in our heads. It made for a full evening. Having usually skipped supper I would have an after-class cup of coffee at the stand across Argyle Avenue, often coinciding with Mauricio, a young Mexican vet with an astonishing trumpet technique. People said he could sight-read anything, even flyshit. Before going on to park cars on Sunset Boulevard he would always eat three incendiary white peppers from the big jar, washed down with strawberry soda, and topped off with a joint as fat as his thumb. He had lost the pinky on his right hand in the war, leaving him the three fingers his valves required. He said it proved God meant him to play the trumpet. But evidently God didn't mean for him to become famous. Like most of the fellow students whose names I knew, he vanished somewhere below the water-line. The fine guitarist Ulysses Livingston, who had recorded with Jazz at the Philharmonic and played for Ella Fitzgerald and Benny Carter, was in Dave's class to learn the new bebop harmony, but even he ended up as an electronic engineer. It's always been hard out there for jazz players.

I didn't have the chops to play bebop, so I was an outsider at Westlake, but a couple of years later I enrolled at San Jose State College as a music major. Having yet to hear Artie Shaw's dictum that "presumption is the mother of a fuckup," I was presuming to lead a small jazz group. I had signed onto the quixotic campaign to "revive" the great jazz of the twenties (as if the records from which I learned it hadn't kept it alive—as they do today). Our quintet, all in our own twenties, was soon magically augmented by the second great teacher of my own little jazz life, the bassist Eino William (Squire) Girsback, a total pro, built like a college linebacker, and equipped with an edgy smile, half sunshine, half sneer. He thought we had possibilities and after we had landed a Friday-through-Sunday gig at a club on San Jose's Cannery Row, he joined us—for peanuts—and stayed for a year. Never mind his new wife, his brand-new son, and a fresh mortgage.

He had his own way of talking. Early on he told us, accurately enough, that the band was presently "not quite adequate to the circumstance." To correct that, he rented (for ten dollars) a large hall in the hills northwest of San Jose. There we convened on a Saturday afternoon, and, in his occult fashion, he gave us an amazing lesson in jazz rhythm. All that afternoon we played only one tune, over and over and over, a very simple one, with chords matching either Duke Ellington's "Stompy Jones" or the Baptist hymn "Just a Closer Walk With Thee." Tempos, he said, were what metronomes measured. What mattered more were what he called "motions," which determined how to attack (or hang back from, or cuddle up to) a tune in a given tempo. Each motion would produce a different "circumstance."

He would wave his hand languidly above his strings to suggest one motion, or do a little grunting strut, or throw a rapid series of right hooks in the air—all these, and more, denoting different ways to play a tune in one unchanged tempo. Then he would demonstrate the motion on the bass, accenting or answering his plucked notes from a large repertoire of vocal sounds. For different tempos he showed us other motions. All of them came out of his body and the looks on his face. After that afternoon the band came together and took off. The club was full. The boss was happy. So was Squire. Before (and during) the Sunday evenings that ended our work week, he began treating us to little feasts: say, five pounds of cracked crab, fresh sourdough bread and unsalted butter, and a few bottles of cold Chablis. He was teaching us how to live, including how to drink and smoke dope "without turning into furniture," as he put it.

When that year finally crashed amid bouncing checks, and we had our employer before the Labor Commission, Squire moved on to Las Vegas to work with the Delta Rhythm Boys. There Louis Armstrong heard him and hired him for his All-Stars. I got a little mileage out of complaining that Louis had stolen my bass player.

When I was through with college I moved to San Francisco, played with a couple of bands there (while teaching English, my day gig). Around 1960, I insinuated myself into my first real jazz *scene,* and gradually became part of the shuffle of sitters-in at an ongoing session on the waterfront. In retrospect it is clear that my own play got better only when I was trying to play unfamiliar music with people better than I. At Pier 23 the musician in charge was a pianist named Bill Erickson. The management gave him just enough money—and it wasn't much—to pay two more musicians on a regular basis, six nights a week. But in San Francisco there were always enough players loose on a given night to guarantee a professional group of up to eight ready to go by 9:30

p.m. at the latest. (Erickson said it got too crazy with more than eight.) Fresh drop-ins would keep it going until 2 a.m., when we would bolt the last of our supermarket gin and disperse into the night. Stanton's Blue Label gin was the only drink Jerome poured musicians free, believing it was all they drank. Erickson kept a little brown medicine bottle of vermouth in his jacket, because Jerome charged you full dollar for a Martini.

Many ingredients combined to make the Pier 23 scene what it was. Havelock Jerome—what journalists used to call *a colorful figure*—had supposedly bought the place with his earnings as a bookie. The crowd might have been assembled by a good casting director: merchant seamen (foreign and domestic), slumming socialites from down the Peninsula, scholarly jazz fans from Berkeley requesting obscure tunes, route men selling pills and joints, dealers in hot merchandise (out of the trunk of his car, one of them sold me a perfectly-fitting black suit I would wear for years), and, rarely, a Musicians Union business agent, looking to bust people. (The session there was one huge infraction.) And those were only the clearly-marked types, along with night people, drifters and drinkers of all descriptions. There were no fights: Jerome kept a sap behind the bar, but never used it. At most a welterweight, he was a master of the bum's rush—magical to see it in action, or merely to hear it: the rush and scrape of shoes, one thud against the door, and another on the sidewalk outside with a grunt; the futile last curse, returned with interest by Jerome.

At Pier 23, styles dissolved, and the caveats of critics were as so much foam on the Bay outside. Erickson ran the shop with great economy, calling tunes—he knew everything—with an eye on who was playing. His rule was simple and bracing: *If somebody knows the melody and somebody knows the chords we can play anything.* I learned all over again to shut up and listen, then try to hold up my end. The talent in the room was usually a cross-section of whoever was around on a given night, including the occasional name, but those like me who had become regulars were never demoted to make room for visitors, except as we chose to be gracious.

Quite a few names dropped in for a drink or to sit in for a set, but they mattered much less than the really good and non-famous professionals you got to know there. Take the trumpetist who had worked for Earl Hines and Charlie Barnet (and who introduced me to the playing of Clifford Brown one afternoon); a magisterial Coleman Hawkins-Ben Websterish tenor saxophonist and import-exporter who dated airline stewardesses; a fine New Orleans-raised drummer who pressed pants all day; a clarinetist who had recorded with Django Reinhardt; a bassist who had played with Charlie Parker, kicked a heroin habit, married a nurse, and now sold rugs in Daly City.

The latter had something in common with Erickson, who had been working cruise ships to Asia during the early fifties when he got his Notice to Report. The drummer in that seagoing trio was supporting the jazziest chemical dependency of those days, and from him Erickson got the notion that if he developed a heroin habit, the Army wouldn't take him. He was right, it wouldn't, but San Quentin did, and kept him for a year. The whole experience, he said, produced in him "a lasting interest in ecstasy," but when he got out, and went to work accompanying exotic dancers in the Tenderloin, he stayed clear of hard drugs, making do for the rest of his life with alcohol, cannily rationed, and a yearly trip into the Berkeley hills to sniff ether with a musician buddy. He knew everything about music, jazz, classical and otherwise. In a college Composition class he had written a plausible Mozart symphony to see how it would sound. He listened closely to every kind of jazz. He liked *form* in pianists. Teddy Wilson had it, he said, and Bud Powell and Horace Silver. He also knew vast tracts of near-useless music, like the complete scores to all the Shirley Temple movies. Now and then he'd call "On the Good Ship Lollypop" or "Animal Crackers in My Soup." Just being around him was instructive.

About 1960 my own tastes and preferences in jazz had widened in a kind of quantum leap. I'd been hearing bebop since I was in high school: now it made sense to me, so I began hearing live the people whose records I was buying: Monk and Gillespie, Rollins and Coltrane, Silver and Blakey and the Adderley Brothers, Miles Davis and Johnny Griffin, Pepper Adams and J. J. Johnson, who played high-speed saxophone parts on the trombone. Let me not overlook a great Count Basie band, playing to packed dance-floors at the Longshoremen's Hall. A whole universe.

When I didn't have to work in the morning I also liked to sit up drinking screwtop wine all night with Erickson after the gig, playing records and inventing bands made up of people we knew, the most irritating in one, the most self-centered in another, but our favorite was made up of people who hated one another. We called it the Kamikaze Band, and when two or more members showed up in the same set at the pier, we would usually swap smiles. When he got married I was his best man. There were just we three, plus a witness we drafted at Berkeley City Hall. That night, I dropped and broke his favorite Bud Powell record. Erickson didn't blink. He said he had it in his head. The marriage didn't work out. In his early forties, Erickson got irreversibly depressed and put his head in the oven. He had most of what it took to make it up above the water-line—all except the ego, the drive, the competitive edge which used to fuel cutting contests. He was a bit of a philosopher, a cooperator, a private smiler.

It was at Pier 23 that I gradually became friends with a musician named Frank Goudie, a giant at six foot seven, in whose hands a clarinet looked like a toy and a tenor saxophone like an alto. Born in New Orleans, he was only recently back in the U.S. after a quarter of a century in Europe and South America. In Paris, he had played and recorded with Django Reinhardt and Coleman Hawkins, and worked all over Europe with jazz groups. His professional nickname was "Big Boy" but friends called him "Tree."

I think we started to be real buddies after I cooked him a pot of *couscous*, the one food he missed after leaving Paris. Goudie believed that *couscous* could cure any digestive problem, and after I told him where he could buy a sack of it cheap, he began eating it every morning for breakfast. In return he led me through the Fillmore district to tiny eateries which served soul food even before anyone called it that. One of our favorites was a bony stew called Monkey Hips and Rice, served by a silent black lady in a blue-and-gold turban. I asked Goudie if he knew what was in it and he shook his head, but afterward, walking back to his place, he said, "Most kitchens there's a cat, but you never do see cats around that place."

If any single person taught me the essential importance of *swinging*, it was he. Goudie would swing hard in any tempo, any key, on any kind of tune. He still spoke English with a French accent, and would lapse into French when balked, but Louisiana lay under it all. When he was pleased it was like a lighthouse going on: *La vie est belle, le morale est bon, est les troupes son fraîches!* He'd heard that somewhere. *Mais ma devise—comment dit on "la devise?"*

"Motto," I said.

"*Yes!* My motto! My motto is, 'Even if I'm wrong, I'm gonna *hit!*'" He was rarely wrong, and never for more than a bar or two, and he always, always hit.

Midway in the Pier 23 years I landed six nights a week at the last functioning dime-a-dance hall in the Bay area, replacing a better man who had burned out on the gig. Musicians still called it the "dime grind" though by then a dance cost a quarter. This was the Rose Room, in deserted downtown Oakland, one flight up from a block of grim bars with names like The Lone Star and The Last Roundup. Each advertised a special on A Shot and A Beer, up or down a nickel from week to week like competing gas stations. Thanks to a civic ordinance there was no drinking at the Rose Room, so the lonely Texas welders and Filipino merchant sailors and divorced salesmen desperate enough to come there would load up at one of the bars, then climb the stairs and buy a strip of tickets.

I'd thought the hostesses might be independent contractors after hours but most were Berkeley grad students and the house rule was Hands Off. No, they didn't need a ride home, thanks. Musicians didn't inspire their confidence. A ghastly decorum prevailed, enhanced by much too much pitiless lighting. A dance lasted between 90 and 110 seconds, a chorus and a half to two choruses of every tune. No "motions" at all, and only two tempos, medium fast and medium slow.

The band was a quartet led by a veteran tenor saxophonist named Henry with a bite like Houdini hanging by his teeth. An electric organist, a drummer and I were his sidemen, but since the union contract required each of us to get fifteen minutes off per hour, we were effectively a trio for all but first and last quarter-hours. It could get dodgy when the organist was on his break, because the drummer had glaucoma, and after he'd had a few pours downstairs he would keep forgetting whether or not he'd put his drops in and stop drumming while he tried to find his eyes with the dropper, leaving Henry and I playing an uneasy duet.

I stuck it out for six or seven weeks. Then, on a pay night (cash), I was mugged across the street by a slender journeyman wearing a stingy-brim, a small knife and a reassuring professional calm. I turned around and dropped my brand-new money behind me as ordered. I had no bridge fare to drive home, and when I told him, he left it on the pavement at my heels. It was almost a pleasure doing business with him. But after that, I handed in my notice. I went back to the pier like a vet fresh from the wars, and Jerome gave me a big glass of Blue Label.

In 1980, living in the Netherlands, I was taken on by a Dutch group energetically committed to keeping alive the music of the postwar New Orleans Revival. It was led by a retired Dutch Army sergeant, who put me in a quasi-military uniform and set me to work in a surprisingly authentic-sounding New Orleans-style street band. Seven of its members also worked in clubs and from March to October at weekend festivals. Lots more live music per capita bought and paid for there than in the U.S.

The sergeant played trumpet and sang, powerfully and with feeling, but he was of that persuasion which believes technique the enemy of sincerity. Despite that handicap, he booked some two hundred gigs a year, indoors and out, for decent money. It took me a couple of years to get into both bands, but the time would come when I would stay alive from what I earned with the La Vida Jazz Band and the Silverleaf Brass Band (both authentic New Orleans names). The sergeant also had the knack, or luck, of hiring superior rhythm sections, without which any band, at any level, is dead in the water. Even when the horns were at odds, the band swung like crazy.

He hired a gangly and baby-faced drummer on the day the kid turned twenty-one. He became a regular, and turned out to be one of the two or three best I would ever play with. But he was coltish, and given to pranks. These didn't go down well with the sergeant, who had whipped so many like him into infantrymen. Once the drummer realized this he got serious about being naughty. He came on a gig, hid a bag of cream puffs behind his bass drum, then ate steadily and messily through the first set, playing one-handed without hurting the tempo. The sergeant didn't notice.

The following gig he appeared with a Walkman in his shirt pocket, a cassette of rock or hard bop in place, and earphones. Whatever the war of tempos in his head he kept us swinging, but this time something gave him away. The sergeant whirled and exploded. Then came the cold war. At that point no one else wanted to lose the drummer, and the drummer wouldn't reform. The sergeant bided his time. Finally came a concert at the civic center in Alphen aan Rijn, where our dressing room was a city office, complete with copy machine. The drummer was lately hurting from severe romantic deprivation. On an intermission he managed to run off a dozen photocopies of his genitalia. Smiling, he handed them out to attractive women leaving after the show. One complained. That was it, the sergeant said, but the band split down the middle. To keep things from falling apart, the sergeant nursed his wrath a bit longer. On a night when one of the pro-drummer members was absent, he called for the vote, won three-to-two, and *then* fired the drummer.

Fairness is a religion among the Dutch. The same kind of stuff has always gone on in the U.S., but here the leader just fires the offender out of hand, as Cab Calloway did Dizzy Gillespie (for shooting spitballs on the stand).

Toward the end of my eight years in the Netherlands I needed a roof over my head and had no money but what I made playing for the sergeant. I was saved by a member of the band, Emile van Pelt. A conservatory-trained French hornist, he played piano for the indoor band and genuinely hot sousaphone with the street band—in either case his harmony and rhythm were invaluable. He offered me a room in a nice upstairs flat occupied by himself and his girlfriend in a pleasant town east of Amsterdam. Thanks to rent control, I could pay my share, eat and drink, and still have a couple of guilders to rub together.

Emile resembled Erickson in his panoramic knowledge of all sorts of Western music. An even better analyst of music, the best I've ever known, he had come to this conclusion: You want respect? Play classical music. Money? Play rock. But if you want fun, play jazz. At Emile and Heleen's place, there was always coffee ready, and a bottle of drinkable cheap Scotch (brand name Cluny), and music playing. Emile was another one of those rare people from whom you learn just by spending time with them. His judgments—on composers, on musicians, on specific tunes—were at once severe and generous. I came to rely more and more on them, and they still make total sense twenty years later.

I also rode to every gig with him in his Skoda sedan. After a few years we were touring more and more, on our own or backing senior musical dignitaries with roots in New Orleans. Belgium, West Germany, Sweden. My last major engagement with Emile (and the sergeant) and a fine new drummer the sergeant had recruited at age fifteen, was in Switzerland at the 1988 Ascona Festival—eleven days of New Orleans-rooted goings on at the edge of the Lago Maggiore, with sidetrips to gigs in Milano.

We were backing a seventy-seven-year-old tenor saxophonist named Sam Lee, born in New Orleans but long since translated to Los Angeles and happiest playing the rough-edged, honking style which Illinois Jacquet made hugely popular in the Sax Battles that highlighted the Jazz at the Philharmonic tours of the forties and fifties. He had his features, "Sam's Boogie" and the very similar "Hi Yo, Silver," one or both of which climaxed our every set. Since we were the two English speakers in the band, Sam and I hung out together, and I sat next to him on the stand.

No one ever demonstrated the Conservation of Energy more convincingly than Sam Lee on the bandstand. At first, I thought he was either putting us on or just resting. In fact, he was asleep. When it was time to sing or play a solo, he was right there. He never missed. Sometimes he snored softly, sometimes not. A man might carry out this charade for a whole set, even a whole night, but not for a week and a half. I though this skill might somehow be related to the marvelously fluid line of his conversation. We talked a lot. Sam always listened when you talked, or seemed to, but his answer might be an account of someone he had known in 1951, or of a dish his wife had cooked the day before he'd caught the plane. The stream of his consciousness never stood still for long.

Finally I asked him about the sleeping on the stand, and this time got an answer. "See, in the old days, we were always on the bus. The one-nighters, you know? And I never did learn how to sleep on the damn bus, so I had to learn to do it on the gig."

Back in L.A., he was a deacon of his church, and when he died, a huge crowd of friends saw him off, complete with a New Orleans-style street band. He was the best example I ever met of that decent, sturdy, reliable competence which characterized so many of his musical generation. Except for a tour of duty with Fats Domino, he had never got anywhere near the top of any iceberg. I'm sure it didn't matter to Sam. But without several thousand Sam Lees, I know there would be no jazz.

A friend bailed me out of the Netherlands by finding me a year's teaching job in Southern California, and even before I got back I was lined up, by phone, with an audition for a uniquely eccentric jazz group in that particular college town. I could never have imagined it. The man who hired me (a brilliant man, a good man, but rhythmically challenged) played the washboard. He said he was trying to be the first *bebop* washboard player in history. He also sang. The self-appointed leader, a philosophy professor and clarinetist, had the habit of keeping approximate time, loudly, with a right-footed goosestep (while seated). This disturbed the washboard player so much that he fitted his glasses with an opaque black shade on the clarinet side so that the goosestep wouldn't throw of his own rhythmic invention. The banjoist (actually a bassist) was my only old friend in the band; the very competent bassist had been rehabilitated and promoted after years in rock bands. I got my tryout in the ceramics lab of the clarinetist's college, and evidently passed.

We had an (unpaid) weekly gig in a local espresso café, and put in occasional appearances at other places, including Jelly Roll Morton's grave, and the Venice Boardwalk, where we dodged roller skaters as we played. The repertoire was a goulash of jazz standards and oddities (to which the washboard player sang his own ingeniously perverse new lyrics), and bizarre numbers by New Age pop bands like Blondie and X (these for a blond singer who would appear from time to time). We also played a few of the simpler Thelonious Monk tunes. When we added a brilliant local electric guitarist (he was curious, and open to new things) the magic was complete. The word *jazz* has described very few stranger ensembles.

Over the intervening seventeen years, this group has morphed into an actual small band playing mainstream swing with a certain élan, if I do say so. Due to death and personnel changes (accidental and deliberate) only the banjoist (now playing guitar) and I remain of the earlier lineup. It is not nearly as quaint and weird as it once was, but it's a lot more musical, and it swings. It's one of the chief joys of our lives, and if I needed reminding it would remind me that—wherever you are in the iceberg—one of the great blessings of jazz is that you never really know what may happen next. If you did, something crucial would be missing.

As for the young man whose trombone I appropriated, he caught up with me half a century later, when I was playing a gig in a railway station café in San Juan Capistrano, where the swallows famously come back to the mission every year. I bought him a drink, and apologized. He is—was—a gentle and forgiving man, but he deserved the last word, and he had it: "That's okay. I couldn't play it either."

Hotel Rex

Looming over the little sewing kit
and the miniature bottles of shampoo
and conditioner, I am a giant—

a king standing before the royal mirror
in an enormous robe of terrycloth.

As a sign of my benevolence,
I will forego coffee
from room service and check out early

before my tiny subjects arrive
to wash their hair and mend their simple attire.

To Posterity

Even before I had arrived on the scene,
Whitman knew I would stand just where he stood
on the edge of the East River
watching the tidal flux and the swoop of gulls,

and maybe you have stood there, too,
among the barrels and the taut wires.
But I would rather know—
assuming you and the city and its rivers

are not covered in ash—
if you like a little wine with your lunch,
is there a view from your study,
and does the neighbor's dog bark at night?

And speaking of the experience of earth,
have you ever risen early
and left a sleeping woman behind
to walk along a beach in the first light

and then returned and told her,
sitting on the edge of the bed
with your hand on her warm shoulder,
what you had seen—

the ruffled clouds,
the grey-green waves and the shorebirds
running over the wet sand,
the amazing, comical speed of their delicate legs?

Petunias

According to the wisdom brewing at the seminar table,
a poem that begins with petunias
should find a way to get away from petunias.

It should deviate from its path,
break the flower-chain of content
transcending botanical considerations altogether.

But sometimes a poem shows
no interest in executing a sudden turn,
swerving off in some unexpected direction

much to the reader's surprise and delight.
Instead, the poem continues happily on its way,
plowing straight down the page

and ends up ending with nothing but petunias,
a row of them along a brick path,
a trowel dropped in the dark soil,

or a vase of them by a window,
the stems bent in the glassy water, why not
a poem with petunias growing from its mouth and ears.

NICOLE COOLEY

Save Beach Elementary

Pascagoula, Mississippi

Do Not Enter the green stucco school,
cyclone fence studded
with debris and memorial wreaths,

monkey bars shadowing
blacktop where hopscotch, four square
still scrawl yellow.

Do Not Touch the dodge ball
under the crepe myrtle tree or
the waterline ringing the building,

boarded windows eyes shut tight
against the flood. Do Not Destroy
this place the sign reads.

Late August, I'm walking
the streets in the Town
of No Children,

and it's true—I don't want
to imagine the children
who drowned here.

An X and an O blurred
in spray paint on a door don't
explain it

and past the recess yard,
along Market Street, sign after sign
stuck in the gutted,

on slabs of foundation,
in stacks of pilings
asking us to save the school.

And everywhere the voices—

Do Not Trespass   Do Not Demo   Do Not Come Here
    Keep Out

New Haven (1972)

"If ever, oh ever a Wiz there was,
The Wizard of Oz is one because—*double-time!*—
because-because-because!" Mania does

liven up a song. We detoured for
candy cigarettes. My old pastime—
I smoked; he sang the entire score.

Dad was well, so he got visitation.
It had been—I'd lost track of time—
a year? He launched into a recitation

of a verse I'd written, and wouldn't stop,
but then he stopped. Later, he made time
with the teenaged waitress at the IHOP;

leafing through a *Playboy* I'd found in the car,
I eavesdropped till it was finally time
to go and Dad paid her and lit a cigar

and drove, like any father, toward home
(my home), jazzed up, bellowing my poem.

After

After the funeral,
after friends and distant relatives departed,
and the house, once again, grew quiet,
we opened closets and bureau drawers
and packed away in boxes dresses, shoes,
the silk underthings still wrapped in tissue.
We sorted through cedar chests of linens and lace,
the quilts she had sewn sitting by the window
on winter afternoons. We gathered
and set aside the keepsakes and the good silver,
and brought up from the coal cellar
jars of tomato sauce, peppers, jellied fruit.
We dismantled, we took down from the walls,
we bundled and carted off and swept clean.
Good-by good-by, we said, closing
the door behind us, going our separate ways
from the house we had emptied,
and which, in the coming days, I would fill
again and empty and try to fill again.

One for the 5-String

You have to tell a story.
—Lester Young, on improvisation

A Saturday night outside town; full moon
risen above the fields, their summer heat
and fragrance drifting through the open doors
of the roadhouse. Inside, I'm sitting-in
with Joe and The Troubadours, a college boy
trying to find the right notes on a pawnshop banjo.
Joe plays fiddle; Jimmy the Dwarf, French harp;
Windy's on guitar. He's wearing the black leather shoes,
the ones with lightning bolts stitched along the sides,
and the lightning bolt socks to match.
By midnight he's got his head thrown back, high-singing
heartbreak songs and honky-tonk over the clamor,
the crowd looking for a good time now
after the week's labor, couples stepping in close,
swaying off into the gleam and shadows of the bar lights.
You have to tell a story, Prez said. Here's mine:
A woman, slow dancing alone by the bandstand,
smiled up at me, her damp face shining.
Honey, she said, take these chains from my heart.
Well, what did I know about women
or the heart's wayward hesitations, dreaming
of those melodies unheard I read about in books.
Lady, I said, I've never even seen you before.
Asshole, she said, I meant the song.

ALICE FRIMAN

Getting Serious

Today I started looking for my soul.
Yesterday it was my keys. Last week,
my brain which I couldn't find, it being out
looking for me, now that I'm getting so old.

First I thought my soul would have gone
back to Greece where she grew so tall and straight,
she thought she was a column. Or back to camp,
being forever twelve and underdeveloped.
Perhaps, being careless, I left her during the 70s
in bed with God knows whom. Or could be
I buried her with my mother—my head not being right—
but that was my heart.

So I went to where I know
I saw her last. Radio City Music Hall.
I'm six, my feet barely brushing the floor,
and the Rockettes start shuffling out, long-
legged and perfect as paper-dolls kicking up
down in a wave. One body with seventy-two knees
chugging like pistons going back in a forever mirror,
same as in Coney Island's Fun House or on Mama's can
of Dutch Cleanser. And my heart flexed in me, a sail,
and I swear I saw it flying out of my chest
spiriting away my giddy soul, ears plugged and tied
to the mast: *I can't hear you I can't hear you.*

The Life and Times of George Van Den Heuvel

What ever happened to George Van den Heuvel,
carbuncled waiter extraordinaire
who hazed me relentlessly the year
I turned sixteen and took my first job as a waitress
at Le Bistro, Lubbock's only bona fide French café?

Why George Van den Heuvel proposed marriage
on my first day was never clear, nor why
he celebrated our engagement with bewildered customers
even after he took my *no* with grace
and offered me one year to change my mind.

Every day on every table I set a vase
that held a single carnation feathered pink with dye
and considered the criteria by which
I might determine whether George Van den Heuvel
was psychotic or just exceedingly bored.

While I wrapped silverware in paper napkins
and sliced the decorated cakes, George Van den Heuvel
folded menus into dust jackets for my textbooks—
papering over Homer's *The Odyssey* to read
The Life and Times of George Van den Heuvel—

and tended to other institutions such as Joke in a Jar,
that glass canister of macaroons he emptied
every shift to insert a handwritten slip.
We fought all year in front of minor characters
with whom I wiped down sticky counters,

and the desperate assistant manager
who cornered waitresses in the walk-in freezer,
and the seven old men who came five nights a week

in flannel shirts buttoned to the neck
to drink coffee and complain there were no donuts,

only Black Forest Cakes and Linzer Tortes
(the phrase *Linzer Torte* alone sent them into stitches).
Sometimes memory feels like a misplaced bistro
around which history grows
its perpetual urban development,

shrinking a *soi-disant* French café in a strip mall
at the edge of a field of grasses,
but whole operas could be composed
on the passions that surged amidst desserts
displayed like jewelry in lit cases.

November

I'd sooner, except the penalties, kill a man than a hawk...
—Robinson Jeffers

The squirrels are up to their nuts in pecans,
And the largesse of the trees
Has made them careless in their comings and goings,
Their carryings and buryings.
Every few blocks there's one
Who zigged just when he should have zagged;
Car-compacted, sometimes their pink lungs
Pop out of their mouths
So it looks like they've been blowing bubble gum.
After a few more days of crushings,
They have been transubstantiated
Into the sacramental wafers
Of the Large Breed Dog Apostolic Church.
I joke in the way we must joke about death
Or wear the rictus of the dead ourselves,
But I'm sad for the squirrels, sad too for the possum
Lying by the streetside oleanders for three days now.
Its size startles: big as a cat and heavy-bodied.
It startles, too, because usually they don't get hit;
They'll turn toward the oncoming car,
Their eyes will light up like phosphorus,
And the car will brake,
Unless the driver doesn't care,
Which must have happened here.
The eyes on the first day were deep black disks
That made me think it must still be alive,
And there seemed to be little muscle tics around the mouth,
But I couldn't bear to prod it with my toe—
If it was alive, I'd have to do something,
And I had nothing near a plan—
So I stared until I was sure it was still.

It has taken these three days for the eyes to close,
Or perhaps it's swelling that has made them seem to close.
I've been taken to task, and more than once,
For dwelling like this on animal death,
But let me tell you a little story,
A little human story.
I'm going back 36 years to a night after 10:00,
And it may even have been a night of this month
Because I remember sycamore leaves
Sidling like crabs on the street.
I was walking my dog.
And there was the tremolo of a screech owl,
And then suddenly a terrible sound,
Like a cat screaming in heat,
Broke into the tremolo,
And both the dog and I bristled
Because both of us knew it was not a cat sound
But a human one.
Around the corner we found a boy,
Three or four years old, in his pajamas,
Howling in panic, a long way from speech.
I took his hand and led him to each of the houses that were lit.
That long ago, people answered their doors even at night,
And finally we found a woman who knew who he was.
His mother was a cocktail waitress
Who started her shift
An hour after the father came home from his shift at the box
     factory.
Her taillights would barely disappear
Before he took off for his night of drinking
Leaving the boy with his eight year old sister.
I didn't know if he had left the house awake
Or had sleepwalked his way out.
The neighbor called the police, who took him home
To the frightened sister—cops at the door;
What a thing for a kid to waken to.
That boy would be a middle-aged man now.
I often wonder what became of him.

Has he gone passive, alone in the dark
With a needle in his arm?
Is he scratching his pimply ass in jail,
Harmed for doing harm?
It's easy to see him like that,
Hard to imagine him as an orthopedic surgeon
Or a sports writer or a nouvelle cuisine chef.
If you lie long enough in misery,
You don't rise from it,
You make more misery to match it,
And even more to surpass it,
And then it becomes a career.
Tell me, when's the last time
You saw a baby squirrel?
See what I'm getting at?
They're kept in the nest
Until they're grown enough to outrun a dog.
Cars, of course, remain the lightning bolt,
The hand of God,
The mystery beyond mystery
Against which there is no defense.

The Lives of Birds

Such shrieking from the scrub jays,
And then I see what's up:
A crow has a half-grown jay pinned on its back
And is hammering like a cartoon
Woodpecker at its breast.
The adult jays force the crow a few feet away,
But the terrified groundling can only manage
A feeble waggle of its feet in air;
It will never right itself again.
I'm glad this morning's walk is solo;
My wife's heart would dissolve at this witnessing,
And it would be a call to action.
I also have the urge to intervene,
But this scene is full of moral pinfeathers.
Jays will spend whole mornings
Trashing each start
Of a robin's nest,
And when their borders are secure,
And the robin has moved to another tree,
They'll bide their time and then eat the robin's eggs,
Or wait a few days longer to devour the nestlings;
Hunger is hunger,
And they will dine, on or off the menu.
But then there's that other fellow
Who sups with much more civility.
While I prune my bonsai at the patio table,
He lands on a chair back,
Blazing his several shades of blue,
Sizes me up correctly,
Then eats from the cat bowl three feet away.
I forget how many seasons we have lived like this,
Not friends exactly, but ruled by tolerance,
And one of us appreciates the other's beauty.
A group of crows is a called a murder,
For reasons a little clearer now,

Yet there's much I admire about them.
They are completely loyal to each other.
One day I heard rallying caws,
And they came one after another from every direction,
All headed for somewhere north of here.
Following on my bike, I found them
Entering a dcodar, the tree a raucous hive,
And still more of them coming,
Until the posse must have numbered eighty,
And then out of the side of the cedar
Shot a red-tailed hawk
So panicked he looked almost awkward in flight,
Driven from a crow's nestlings
By a murder of numbers.
After he was gone, the caws ceased,
And the dark wings flapped to their outlying trees,
On call for the next calamity.
And crows are problem solvers:
One slammed a plastic-wrapped bundle
Again and again on the pavement
Until the wrap broke open
And the half burrito was his, *con mucho gusto*.
Sometimes a new bird,
Like the vermillion flycatcher, startles me,
And I write it into my life list with sadness
Because I think the first and last sighting
Could be one and the same.
The Aztecs celebrated with a special awe
Flowers and birds,
The flowers adding the colors of their butterflies,
And those flowers of the air, the quetzals,
And the flying jewels, hummingbirds.
The thought of a life, a world, without birds
Is like a death to dreaming.
But enough of life's little extinctions…
Let me celebrate the newest mockingbird in the yard.
The mockingbird, who seems born to entertain
And harms nothing but a life's supply of bugs.
This one is a Frenchman; I know this by his accent

As he calls all day long to his lady love:
Brigitte, Brigitte, Brigitte.
I hear nothing coming back from her,
But my lady love has answered for thirty-eight years now.
It has begun to dawn on both of us
That we are among those rare birds
Who mate for life.
I try a call to Brigitte, too, from the front porch:
Answer him; you could be the singular light
That floods all of his songs.
And then I call to him:
Pierre, Pierre, I wish you *bon chance;*
I wish you my luck, *mon ami.*

On the Transmigration of Butterflies and Other Events

For five years my father's body lay abandoned at the Tri-State Crematory in North Georgia. Along with 333 other bodies, his remains were recovered in 2002.

He says

he's been pretty disappointed
with the whole thing. Like all of us
he had heard of so many possibilities.
Like the white light churning at the tunnel's end.
Now that was a good one. It sounded good.
Also the one about

the annihilating face of god
that doesn't annihilate. Instead
it just sends its beams, beaming.

Or the greenest

and best people in a green field.
Or a boat ride taken for the price of a coin.
Even the slow wafting of a pig's filth, the soul
settling into the beautiful life of swine . . . .

But for him it was different.
In his mind of morphine
he gave new words to the darkness
that wrapped him over and over—each layer
claiming its birthright as it turned—each sheet
pulled tighter against his arms.

And suddenly without wings
he found himself here, or maybe not here,
or something resembling being not here,
saying things beneath the trees he shouldn't say.

Self-Portrait

Here in North America we do not experience
an atmosphere of butterflies. They do not fill the air
with such camaraderie that the hills burn orange and yellow
with filtering wings. So on Christmas morning

I offer him the old camera back—
the Leica with the fancy zoom lens. His fingers quiver
whitely as he holds the machine close, clattering
dials and levers and then turning it on himself.

Portrait of a smile in a bad hour. Still-life
with sockets and bone . . . and then all day
my father clicks the things he sees:
this branch changes in the wind and light,

this mockingbird wears different white sleeves.
By late afternoon, propped against a pine,
he's shooting a cold blaze over the angling lake.
Eventually a few stars rise from that red.

Here in North Georgia we do not experience
the moon falling down. Things being what they are.
It does not dive flapping into this lake
like a blasted albatross.

That Winter

In the hundred days I lived in a trailer in Ithaca, New York,
I thought unceasingly of that other Ithaca, wine-dark, beset,
a place from which to start from, maybe to come home to
in some eventuality undreamed of. I cleaned factories
for a guy named Ben who wanted to make movies
and whom I secretly loved (The van was small. Ben climbed
ladders and dropped the spent florescents down to me,
and I caught their shanks with the palms of my hand,
and nothing, ever, was broken, and it was like a dance,
and Ben wondered why I was always cheerful). It was
winter the whole time, white or whitening, never quite beautiful.

Prayer for a Sick Cat

It is not the fall of Nineveh.
Not the sliding of the earth,
the clashing of the icy stars.
Nothing as bad as that.

It is the silence, now,
of a little black cat.
The bowl where he ate.
The chair where he sat.

He's curled in a ball
on the laundry basket.
The cat-nip mouse and the
window sill have begun to grieve.

Bad spirits and good,
someone's always tugging at your sleeve.
My turn tonight. See what a tiny thing this is.
A rag of fur, a rumble.

Let him live, for someone's sake.
He must have made you laugh one time,
singing his song, taking his tumble.
Close the fire-colored cat door

between tonight and the coming day.
I think you have let for a while
enough of the nectar drip away.
Kindle the eye-fire. Let him stay.

The Helmet

Perhaps someone was watching
a mud turtle or an armadillo
skulk along an old interminable footpath,
armored against sworn enemies,
& then that someone shaped a model,
nothing but the mock-up of a hunch
into a halved, rounded, carved-out
globe of wood covered with animal skin.
How many battles were fought before
bronze meant shield & breastplate,
before iron was fired, hammered & taught
to outwit the brain's glacial weather,
to hold an edge? God-inspired,
it was made to deflect a blow
or blade, to make the light pivot
on the battlefield. Did the soldiers
first question this new piece of equipment,
did they laugh like a squad of Hell's Angels,
saying, Is this our ration bowl for bone meal
& gore? The commander's sunrise
was stolen from the Old Masters,
& his coat of arms made the shadows
kneel. The ram, the lion, the ox,
the goat—folkloric. Horse-headed
helmets skirted the towering cedars
till only a lone vulture circled the sky
as first & last decipher of the world.

The Warlord's Garden

He has bribed the thorns
to guard his poppies.
They intoxicate the valley
with their forbidden scent,
reddening the horizon
till it is almost as if
they aren't there.
Maybe the guns guard
only the notorious
dreams in his head.
The weather is kind
to every bloom,
& the fat greenish bulbs
form a galaxy of fantasies
& beautiful nightmares.
After they're harvested
& molded into kilo sacks
of malleable brown powder,
they cross the country
on horseback,
on river rafts
following some falling star
& then ride men's shoulders
down to the underworld,
down to rigged scales
where moneychangers
& gunrunners linger
in their pistol-whipped hush
of broad daylight. No,

now, it shouldn't be long
before the needle's bright tip
holds a drop of woeful bliss,
before the fifth horseman of the Apocalypse
gallops again the night streets of Europe.

The Night Life Is for You

Here, on the boulevard of run-
amuck dreams, each stamped
with a doll-like face you half-
recognize as yours, the neon
displays its chilly, self-
possessed light.
But the lips on the billboards
are raspberry cream. They say
Buy me or Be me, you
can't tell. You're confused
like mad again, in this night
of mixed blessings spiked
with a ripe curse, that line
you fall for every time.
You'll drive these streets
in a trance after your death
crying I'm still here!
but now you get out and walk.
This pale, feverish presence
inside your life is you,
and those are loud strangers
gripping beers. But why die,
ever, while stores shout out
their bargains, hot CD's,
and one can gaze at the bodies
who've stopped dancing now
and stand about jaggedly
because the doorways
of rock clubs pumped them
into open air? No doubt about it,
all this is for you.
Some Doo Wop tune
on the airwave says the night's

thousand shifting eyes
are on the watch. You guess
two of them are yours.
Tonight Mr. Good
or Bad might pluck you
from the crowd.
There's some place you're
supposed to be, some fun
you're supposed to have.
It's fate, your fate, and it's open
twenty-four hours.

DAVID MASON

In the Meadow

The meadow hears everything—or does it?
Perhaps the short-haired girl up to her knees
in grass is the one who takes it all in.
She's skin and wide eyes, alertness and hurt,
as if she can remember the fireflies
sparking on some future night, the voices
saying *I want to be like this forever.*

As if the night were flesh, the grass and shadows
and air perspiring, birds leaning from boughs
to hear such whispering and such despair.
The meadow's an echo: *Listen. Listen.*
They go on, they go off, sad little lights
of summer. What future do they die into?

Is it the same future she can almost see
through her skin? She is so small, so abandoned
under the fathering trees, all time at the root.
The meadow talks to its twin across the water:
I want to be like this forever. I want...
The girl grows to a woman listening there
through touch through blood through everything
    she knows.

Energy

For Dewey Huston

Tell me again about the butterflies,
old friend of my father, bringer of tales,
the gully, mossy rocks of the streambed,
a cool breeze off the glacier high above,
and suddenly butterflies everywhere
as if the air you breathed were blossoming.

I've seen so many things, you said. I wish
I could write them down. And when my brother died
you were the alpinist and engineer
who had an explanation where he'd gone,
waving a hand in air. It's energy,
you said. That energy must still be somewhere.

Ah, but the real life is never written down,
and who could understand the butterflies—
that there were so many, so surprisingly?
Tell me again, old friend, and I will try
to catch the light, the flavor of the air
like moss, like distant ice, like clear water.

Furlough

for lunch he made
her sweet peas
with milk and butter
her favorite—
and after school
he taught her lessons
in French kissing
until the grandmother
caught her snuggled
in his lap fingering
combat ribbons and stripes
the smell of aftershave
and tobacco safe and after
all what did she know
when she was pulled
away and grandma said
you're too big for that mess
and him the one she called
daddy like her mama did
stroking his mustache
and saying 'ain't nothing to it'—
but what he doesn't say: how
you're out there so long
with life coming cheap
and death at your elbow
you forget what hurts
and what scars you forever

Crossing the Rubicon at Seventy

we do not know the name
of the river that roils
beneath us until we arrive
at its shores—until we give
reason to pass along or stay
there where waters sound
like uncut jewels swirling
in a tide pool—until the little
boats we've made fold like kites
in a storm—until we've come
to that point where turning mid-
stream is outside reason and staying
lays sour on the tongue—know
you have shaped a raft before
floating with the current toward
another long day's journey—know
you have yet another reason
to reinvent yourself before
you take the last route home

Against Etymology

At dark, I make a homesick
says a Japanese exchange student
in my wife's ESL class,
writing how much he misses
his family, his girlfriend,
a certain café in Kyoto.
I suggest tutoring. But that night,
it feels strangely fitting
after our second bottle of wine
to cap the red pen
bleeding cursive
from her palms and lead her
into the bedroom. Let's make sleep,
I whisper—and we lie
still sheathed in our clothes,
two bodies fused like Latin roots
while a full moon
the color of vegetable stock
unfurls its approval,
shimmering through curtains
that shadow us—yes—
like clapping paper fans.

The Red Shoes

Pulling out government coupons for the first time
In a Krogers twelve blocks from her walk up
So the bagboys and cashiers and seniors
Browsing tabloids would all be strangers,
She's slow motion through and past their stares.
She feels every nuance of her body
As a tense repressed trembling, a calculated
Conscious stepping, just as much a dance
Of desperation as that solo waltz
Around the brass pole in the gentleman's club
She'd never do. Nothing said, but the gist
Of the story bared, Lonnie gone and the car
After missed payments, no degree, nurses aide
Not enough for even store brand soup,
And those looks from everyone contribute
To the scrutiny she's already put herself under,
The wondering what's become of her
Least dashed hope, like that man in the dominion
Of his cubicle at the welfare office
Teasing out the names of men who stayed
The night. She's been made small. She's been cut down
To size like that little girl with the red shoes
Told by the angel she'd dance for all
The vain children, dance through the moonlight
And the villages and the dark dreamy woods,
Who never stopped even when she stood begging
The executioner not to lop off her head,
Then letting him harvest her feet instead.
So she seasons her sauce with damp salt
From her own eyes and her back to her son
In his proud sneakers and best sullen thirteen
Because he won't ever know she's good
As dirt, a polite little clot of nothing

Waiting while that laughing bureaucrat
Carried on in front of her long and personal
On the phone. *Approved* was the word he used,
Meaning yes to those two sacks which would last
However long they must like the whole
Brutal fiction of grace, the executioner
Giving the girl crutches after the axe.

Beauty

He entered the sty, and she cringed. She'd always
Remember him, a beast with black hair
And blue eyes, a young German, and the sound
Of screeching ducks and gunshots in the barnyard
Where treacherous neighbors had gossiped
Away the good frightened family who'd stashed her
And hers like livestock with souls, butchered then
Or driven off in a truck. Comprehending
Her face, his rifle still trained, he lowered
His stare to the straw laced mud. He left,

And with this beautiful act became like a pig
That had swallowed a diamond: whoever
Slit him open would wonder where it came from.
She knew what she rarely said afterwards,
That he looked like a boy she could have liked,
Like the tall coachman who let her ride
With the crates once on his flat wagon
Or the rabbi's son she'd daydreamed kissing
In the lilacs behind the gymnasium, a real prince
At whom she could never so much as smile
Without having her decency questioned...

And so the curse is lifted, the one
Who sprayed their blood in the usual ritual
All over the rotted stoop hasn't urged them
To kneel in his grunting, accurate tongue
Because he's in here with her and in love,
Transformed by it, if only for an instant.

TOMAS Q. MORIN

Dumb Luck

There are some things I should tell you
beforehand: I was born on a bed
covered quickly with a quilt. I stepped

my bare feet into the new world
of a lamp-lit room in the country.
Because of a broken driveshaft we stayed,

my mother and I, among the witch-hazel
straddled houses and the buzzard-heavy
poles rising upward like wooden angels.

She had meant to rest on the bleached
linens of the Sisters of Mercy
hospital, if only I had not come early

I might have been named Olaf
or Sven after one of the three doctors
in town. Why does any of this matter

you wonder, what is the point
of unwinding the threads of this life
I will never have? My mother wanted

a daughter so at five I dressed flowers
with my hair and answered to Margaret
as she watched my face darken

with all the coming furies of boyhood.
If they had conceived me sooner
I might now remember my father

taking his streaked hand to my back
and lifting me into the stunned air
of April, although common sense suggests

I wouldn't have remembered the moment
nor his face or the light rain tapping
its fingers on our shingled roof

like a deaf man pounding Chopin
away on the keys of an unstringed piano
because he believes what he was told,

that there is joy in our sheer movement
of a thing from A to B, that a sound
made realizes its purpose when it fills

a silence because that is what we do
when we are born. We waken and cry
to the silent walls and a radio gone hush,

to the earthbound rooster and hens
bent in the yard because we are finally
in the world we always said we wanted.

JOAN MURRAY

The Gardener's Wife

That summer in the mound of sand
someone left beside the cesspool lid,
my father managed to grow a watermelon—
it's not what you're picturing—maybe not even edible,
the size of a softball, but, hell, it was a watermelon,
and, all year round, the man worked two jobs in the City,
and only came out on summer weekends, but he knelt down
and planted it. From a seed. With a kid's shovel.
And every weekend he tended it by hand,
he put up twigs and twine, he weeded, watered, the way
God must have done before he brought in
the gardener and the gardener's wife
and everything went wrong.

My father said he "got a kick out of it" —
he liked to say that about lots of things—
not just watermelons, cats and dogs, his children even.
My mother watched him, watched the way
he knew how to be happy over nothing,
and on Mondays when he got the train back to the City,
she would take her tools out of the outhouse that we now
had to call "the shed": her trimmers and pruners,
her clippers and scythe—and the pole with the saw-toothed
    hook

that could reach up and take down anything.
But she didn't need them for that watermelon,
I mean, someone could just pick it up
and chuck it into the bushes like a ball.

Family Dollar

The New Choice Pregnancy Testing Kits
are hung along the ramp-up to the register.
The woman ahead of me would pass hers
with flying colors. She's huge and sighing,
the kids in her cart keep eying my candy.
I recognize the cashier—she's the girl who used to
work at the Video Cave that closed.
We saw her one time after that—at the go-kart place.
She told us she'd moved away, she had won
some kind of scholarship. And was going to start
college in Syracuse. We watched her
boyfriend race her around the track,
he made her howl with such abandon
when he rammed her.

The house just east of the go-kart place
caved in a month ago. It had been peeling
and boarded up for years. When I'd drive by,
I used to say, *I bet there's something
good in there.* Then one night last July,
I watched three guys come out, they were
carrying the stairs. But who do you call
if you see a thing like that, where do you
start—do you just say, *Send a cruiser right away,
I just saw someone taking a flight of stairs?*
I wonder if she'll remember me—I remember
she was smart. The lines here take a lifetime,
but it's easy to fill your cart. When everything
is next to nothing.

from Archangel

The following excerpts are from *Archangel,* a hybrid work that takes as its center the unnamed "monster" in Mary Shelley's *Franken-stein.* In Shelley's book (so very different from the movies) the "monster" learns to read by overhearing cottagers giving lessons to a foreigner. Subsequently he reads many books—including *Paradise Lost,* Volney's *Ruins of Empire,* and Plutarch's *Lives*—all in an effort to try to understand this strange race that made and yet shuns and fears him. In this section, the "monster," still alive in the 21st century, remembers back to when he first encountered Mary, a child of nine sitting by her mother's—Mary Wollstonecraft's— grave, and how, over a period of weeks, he read many books to her and she listened. She keeps this secret from everyone she knows, until, years after Percy Shelley's death and the deaths of all but one of her children, she writes of what passed between her and the "monster" to her half-sister Claire Clairmont. The "monster" is able to see what Mary's writing to Claire, as she comes to him in recurrent visions—her hand appears before him, out of thin air, writing. In these excerpts, it's been many years since he's had visions of her, and he's startled and unsettled by their return. The monster's voice is presented in regular font; Mary's is in italics.

*

For so many years I tried not to think of her. Or thought of her only as Claire's sister—hazy as through dust storms or smog. I didn't want her to come back. But she's come back.

Dear Claire,
  Now that we live apart and I don't see you face to face anymore, now that all but one of my children have died, and your Allegra has died, maybe I can tell you...but why do I even want to tell you?
  I was a girl when he came to me. This was before Shelley. Before France, Italy, any of it. I would go to her grave, sit there wondering what it would be like to have a mother.

~~I think I have a fever now I think I~~ Truth burns itself up or goes suddenly, horribly cold; it seems there's no neutrality, no balance. (Though that's not what they taught us—I think of Socrates with his measured, steady questions.)

And when I try to feel what thinking is, it's not a series of faithfulnesses but of betrayals, treasons, crumblings. (Remember the ruins at Luna?) There's so much extremity in us, outside of us...and we call it the ordinary, we call it...

~~I have become a shallow~~

This is ordinary: I was a body coming out of another body that died. That died because of my body. This is ordinary: famine, oppression, slavery, carnage, misunderstanding, hatred, love, sun, hostility, squalor. Why do we think the ordinary is benign, why do we...

I would sit there like an idiot by her grave, waiting—for what? I was eight, then nine. Afternoons, some nights...

Thought a violent thing to me, in me (though I kept this mostly to myself). I still feel this, that thinking is a violent act. The smoothness of skin a kind of lie.

When I heard rustling in the bushes, I wasn't afraid. I'd been sitting there for hours, as usual. He stepped mildly toward me, one large hand over most of his face, his head bowed above hunched shoulders.

But maybe I should stop this right now, say nothing more. So why sign my name at all, and still I sign it—

Your sister,

Mary

But I don't want to think about this. Why must I think about this now?

*

Claire,

...I sat there in Saint Pancras Graveyard. The end of summer. The River Fleet moving sluggishly nearby.

(I don't understand stillness, I was thinking—I remember this clearly—thinking, what could be odder than stillness though it's everywhere? Rock. Bone. Knife. Death. Table. My brain ached as I thought this...I was nine...)

He moved very slowly, his chin pressed down and inward where it met his left shoulder.

This is the cemetery of St. Pancras, I said to myself, and St. Pancras is the Patron Saint of Children, but he couldn't be St. Pancras, his head's still attached, and he's too old. Yet he didn't seem like other humans.

Black lips and yellow eyes. Long black hair.

For weeks he came to me. Mostly he stayed hidden in the bushes and would speak almost nothing of himself. Not even when I asked. Read to me from books. Seemed to know who I was.

It's the ordinary that frightens—water, rock, stillness, absence, faces. Thriving gardens. Anchors. Skin.

For weeks I listened as he read.

*

Claire,

Remember when we kept our journals?—

"Tuesday Eighth Letter from Fanny—drawing lesson—walk out with Shelley to the south parade. Read Clarendon and draw-in the evening work & S reads Don Quixote *aloud."*

That was October, 1816. Fanny died the next day. What was I doing when she died?—reading the memoirs of Princesse de Barreith? Drawing? Walking alone or with Shelley? Such ordinary things—

"Wednesday 23rd Write Walk before breakfast. Afterwards write and read Clarendon. Shelley writes & reads Montaigne—In the evening read Curt. & work—Shelley reads Don Quixote *aloud." Days like that. Remember? But not a scrap of writing survives from the years I was a child. So much I didn't tell you—*

Yet I criticized you for being melodramatic, for your "Clairmont Style"—your conviction that some unworldly being was moving through your room disarranging things. And all the time I kept from you what I'd seen when I was nine...

He stepped out of the bushes, partly shielding his face with his hand. He seemed a hurt presence. A presence somehow ashamed.

It's the ordinary that frightens: a plain white envelope, a sunny day in the mountains, reading, thinking, looking at a newborn's skin. The words: "infant," "Monday," "Leghorn," "July," frighten me.

When I was nine: stillness, trust, my own bed, thinking, frightened me.

I felt no need to turn from him.

I asked his name. "I don't have one," he said.

That seemed to me an extraordinary thing. I couldn't decide if it was wonderful or horrible, to have no name like that, yet to be a creature of language, a creature using words.

Why had no one named him? And un-named like that, did he know an alone-ness much worse than my own?

He held a book in his hands. I could tell he didn't want me to look into his face. How does one calm another's shame? Then he stepped back into the bushes, head still deeply bowed, and started in a gravelly, hushed voice, to read.

*

I thought she must have run away. Though when I'd stepped from the bushes she'd seemed calm, unfrightened, even curious, wouldn't she have quickly reconsidered and then fled?

Back within the bushes' cover, I read out loud as I often did to calm myself. I kept many books with me by then:

"In France they have a dreadful jail, the Bastille. The poor wretches who are confined in it live entirely alone; have not the pleasure of seeing men or animals; nor are they allowed any books.—

They live in comfortless solitude. Some have amused themselves by making figures on the wall; others have laid straws in rows. One miserable captive found a spider; he nourished it for two years; it grew tame, it partook of his lonely meal. But when the warden learned of this, he crushed the spider. The prisoner looked round his dreary apartment, and the small portion of light which the grated bars admitted only served to show him that he breathed where nothing else drew breath."

*

"Loveliest of what I leave behind is sunlight,
and loveliest after that the shining stars, and the moon's face,
but also cucumbers that are ripe, and pears, and apples."

*

"We are not as hardy, free or accomplished as animals."
"Before begging it is useful to practice on statues."

123

"I threw my cup away when I saw a child drinking from his hands at the trough."

"The greatest beauty of human kind is frankness."

*

"I have just completed a forty-two day voyage around my room. The fascinating observations I made and the endless pleasures I experienced along the way made me wish to share my travels with the public..."

*

Claire,

He read and I listened. The river rough and muffled in the background. Dull leaf-sounds rustling underneath his voice. My fingers picking at pebbles in the dirt. This was before "must go into town for pins / sealing wax / spy glass," before "buy mourning and work in the evenings," before "I am ill most of the time" and "the watery surface was blank," before "at half past three nothing remained but a quantity of blackish looking ashes mingled with pieces of white and broken fragments of bone..." *I don't even remember why I crossed that out. This was before "my Book dedicated to Silence—"*

I came to realize that some of what he read had been written by my mother. In the extreme...in the mind's farthest corners... *I don't know how to explain this. Sometimes I glimpsed his face, but mostly not. A few times I found some scraps of paper he'd dropped in the bushes: "Clerval who's left for the east," one read. But I'm getting ahead of myself...*

So many years since I've seen you.

Your sister,

Mary

*

Those days in the graveyard I read from whatever I could find—food-stained books lifted from trash cans, newspapers, stray pages left on benches.

"The Emperor Ling Ti, who reigned circa 170 A.D. felt that nothing was too good for his favorite dog. The animal, undoubtedly born under a lucky dog star, was given the official hat of the Chin Hsien grade, the highest rank of the time. The hat was eight and three-quarter inches high, and ten inches in circumference."

"Yao, the famous legendary Emperor of China's Golden Age, is said to have been born with eyebrows of eight different colors."

"In Chinese thought, spiritual intelligence—thought itself—emanates from the heart which is pierced by a number of clear 'eyes' or apertures."

"Why is our fancy to be appalled by terrific perspectives of a Hell beyond the grave?—that Hell is here in the lash that strikes the slave's naked sides, in the poor too sick to eat their sour bread..."

"...although I hear people say 'Moses meant this' or 'Moses meant that,' I think it more truly religious to say 'Why should he not have had both meanings in mind, if both are true? And if others see in the same words a third, or a fourth, or any number of true meanings, why should we not believe that Moses saw them all?"

Sometimes I read from her mother's words that formed in the air in front of my eyes, appearing as from nowhere:

"So much knowledge is partial, conjectural. I'm writing to you from the North—from a place I don't understand—this village of steep rock named Rusoer where the houses are crowded in under the cliffs. Wooden planks serve as walkways. When I leave these wild shores what am I returning to?—How will I live?—I want to understand what Liberty is... Sometimes I imagine Fanny Blood's still alive, rendering her botanical drawings for Curtis's Flora Londinensis. Making her living that way. And that she and I could live together.—The child and I sail back to England in the morning..."

*

Claire,

Lord Dillon once said to me, "I'm puzzled because you seem in no way at all like your writings." But the outward is so little of anything. Those days in the graveyard why should I have been afraid? What did it matter what he looked like? And anyway his manner wasn't threatening, though sometimes his voice grew taut and I felt a kind of pestilence spread inside my brain, an acrid warning. As if he and I were all that was left in a world that had destroyed itself. Everything in ruins. The air a barren plain between us, and I felt a chill, a barrier, a recoil. Not wanting to be left only with him. But then he'd start to read again, and the sense of plague would quiet back inside me.

Do you remember that locked box I carried to France when Shelley and you and I ran away? Inside were the few scraps of paper from the graveyard, the ones he'd dropped in the bushes or the grass. I never knew if he'd left them on purpose. "Clerval who's left for the east" one said, and then there were these: "unable to endure the aspect of the being he'd created" / "the wondrous power that attracts the needle" / "inside his laboratory" / "oppressed by a slow fever" / "dejection never leaves him" / "that I might infuse a spark of being into the lifeless thing at my feet" / "I knew nothing of the science of words or letters" / "this trait of kindness moved me."

And a few more:

"my life was indeed hateful to me"

"by such slight ligaments are we bound to prosperity or ruin"

"to seek one who fled from me"

"vast and irregular planes of ice which had no end"

The handwriting was large, dark, crude, as if written with a branch or twig.

Some nights I'd lie awake imagining a plague covering the earth, and I'd wonder why I couldn't stand the thought that he and I might be the last ones alive—why didn't I want to be left with him?—even though when I listened to him read a comfort fierce as burning sand came into me.

*

Claire,

I kept imagining that he and I were the only ones left alive. His gravelly voice a spider's web which instead of viciously entrapping created against the air a refuge of intersecting lines, a kind of dwelling. I lived within that voice, its stories. And still I couldn't stand the thought of being left with him. Sometimes I imagined hurting him, seeing him cry. ~~Why does the mind disfigure itself why does it~~*...Imagined telling him I hated his voice, his yellow eyes, that he was a disgusting aberration of nature, nothing anyone could ever love. I'd picture his shoulders heaving as he sobbed. Imagined throwing a stick at him or stones. For awhile this comforted me. But why would the thought of hurting him comfort me? I waited each day for him to come—*

Beneath the threatening thoughts a calm so pure nothing could rip it.

*

Claire,

Sometimes I'd imagine I was the only one left alive, then try to feel whether I'd miss him. That hidden, companionable voice...all the stories he brought me, the ideas, the ways of thinking...All the buildings around me still intact—mansions, palaces, libraries, hospitals, hovels, all of them empty but still standing. And I washed up on the narrow shore that was myself, only myself. There was no hope of finding anyone alive, the plague had wiped everyone out, and yet I went into a painter's shop and with paint and brush left messages on walls—"Friend if you're alive come find me in ___" (though I had no friend in mind). And I wrote messages on paper scraps, left them on benches, tucked them into windowsills and doors...

At those times the words I'd heard him read out loud came back, but scrambled, rearranged for this new world emptied of all human breath but mine—:

"To have been born emanates from thought itself;" "each outcry almost imperceptible;" "each damaged design..."

I'd lie in my bed like that, thinking. And then I'd think how it might feel to be like him, alone behind those bushes. Was he angry? Scared? What did he want what did he dream of? And what to make of the world when every impulse is infected with recoil?—

*

Claire,

Over time I brought him things, biscuits, chocolate, some bread. Sometimes I imagined we were friends. But often he felt more like a kind of infection to me than anything else—something awful that I'd caught—that burned me yet I didn't want it to stop—. And even though I didn't fear him, I came to believe I sensed beneath that steady reading voice something I began to tell myself was hatred. Was it hatred of me? Years later when I got smallpox it was as if that hatred was finally writing on my face. Scrawling all over it. That it had been waiting all those years—brewing, taking root, increasing. That he'd planted it somehow, those hours in the graveyard. My ugly, ruined face. I remember walking through the streets glad, finally, to be damaged in that way. The harm visible, overt. The disgusted looks of strangers. Lowered or averted eyes. The giddy justice of it then. Did he hate my fresh-scrubbed skin, the fact that I had a bed to return to every night? Yet he read to me such wondrous things, so why did I even think of hatred? Why did I dream of guillotines, of shredded, mud-stained dresses? Corpses. Atrocities. Bodies floating face-down in the river. Guns. Sabers. Severed limbs—

*

And still I read to her. Week after week of rustling pages. The hush of the river. Clicking of pebble against pebble in her hand. Yet always that vague uneasiness, like chipping at a wall I had no right to touch. (Even in her mother's name a wall. Stone crafted into walls.)

In my mouth the threatened shelter of each word—

Outlaws, vagabonds—chained yet wildly tender, weirdly free—

My voice for hours on end from the bushes, she listening from the other side:

"Curse on all laws but those which love has made."

*

"Ideas are to the mind nearly what atoms are to the body. The whole mass is in perpetual flux; nothing is stable or permanent."

*

"An infinite number of thoughts passed through my mind in the last five minutes. How many of them am I now able to recollect? How many of them shall I recollect tomorrow? Some of them may with great effort and attention be revived; others obtrude themselves uncalled for; and still others are perhaps out of reach of any power of thought to reproduce, as having never left their traces behind them for a moment. If the succession of thoughts be so inexpressibly rapid, may they not pass with so delicate a touch as to elude forever...?"

*

(I'd lost my Crusoe, which was, in any case, missing its last fifty or so pages. I could no longer read of making tools and planting corn and finding Friday...couldn't tell her or myself what happened to them, how they'd fared...)

*

"Kue-lin-fu contains three very handsome bridges, each one more than a hundred paces in length and eight paces in width. The women are also very handsome and live in a state of luxurious ease, as the city possesses much raw silk and exports large quantities of ginger and galangal. The city is well-known for it species of domestic fowl that has no feathers, its skin being clothed in black hair and resembling the fur of cats. This fowl's eggs are of a pale-rose or violet color, and are said to taste of rose-petals mixed with fresh rain."

*

"When thou cam'st first
Thou strok'st me, and made much of me; wouldst give me
Water with berries in it; and teach me how
To name the bigger light, and how the less,
That burn by day and night: and then I lov'd thee,
And showed thee all the qualities of the isle..."

Quiet

The air outside was warm and wet, like breath. Feeling the breeze on his face, the baby stopped crying and looked up at the sky. I turned him around and leaned him against my chest, holding him with one hand curled under his arms, the other cupping his bottom. He gently kicked his legs, as if he were dangling them in water. I walked barefoot across the front lawn toward the shrubbery. The baby's mouth gaped, a thread of saliva stretching from his chin to my arm. I sat down next to a patch of shade under the shrubbery. I made a nest of leaves and pine straw and laid the baby on it. He watched the gemlike glints where light seeped through the clutter of branches, his eyes round. It was quiet beneath his leafy canopy, with just a hint of breeze flustering the grass. After a while I brushed myself off and went back inside, closing the front door behind me.

It was my twenty-third birthday. The baby was almost two months old. I had been sitting with him in the brown corduroy chair in front of the window waiting for Daniel to get home. Daniel had promised to leave work early so that he could cook my favorite meal, macaroni and cheese, and bake me a chocolate cake. His dad and his younger brother Stephen were coming over later to celebrate with us and see the baby. The baby had finally nodded off, his lips still wrapped around my nipple. Outside, the late afternoon sun churned in a cloudless sky. A black cat snoozed under the shrubbery near the window, stretched out on its back. Even the bugs were quiet.

I shut my eyes for a moment. When I opened them, the brown corduroy chair was an old man's hand, the baby and I cradled in his wrinkled palm. I peered over the side of the hand. There was nothing underneath us, just a carpet of sky, the grey green of air expecting storms. When the fingers began closing into a fist, I opened my mouth to scream. I awoke, and the phone was ringing. The baby immediately commenced his wailing, lips taut, gums glistening, tongue quivering under a torrent of displeasure. The cat beneath the shrubbery stretched and yawned, its back curved exquisitely towards the sky. It padded into the sun, crossed the street, and vanished under the neighbor's car.

"How long has he been at it?" Daniel shouted over the phone line.

"Pretty much all day, same as usual."

"You poor thing. Is he hungry?"

"I don't think so," I shouted back. "I think this is his personality."

The baby flailed his arms like a desperate boxer, head thrashing side to side. His hair was brown as dust except for a ribbon of blond where a monk's tonsure would be.

I put the tip of my index finger inside the baby's mouth, to encourage him to suck. He cried harder. "Where are you? It's five-fifteen," I said.

"I have to rewrite a brief. I can't make it home as early as I thought."

"But it's my birthday." I did not bother to yell.

"I know, I'm sorry. It's for that client we went out to dinner with, right before you got pregnant. Remember him, the one who said you looked like his daughter?"

"The filthy rich one."

"Right." Daniel was smiling, I was sure of it. He liked when I remembered his clients. "I won't be long, don't worry." After saying he loved me, he paused a moment, then hung up.

I started to cry. For a few seconds the baby stopped his screeching. Then he took a deep breath and redoubled his efforts. Soon he had succeeded in drowning me out completely, his grief operatic. I squeezed out a few more tears and gave up.

"You win," I said, but he didn't seem to care.

I looked out the window. Droplets of light sprinkled the patch of shade recently vacated by the cat. I imagined the quiet beneath the shrubbery. The baby roared, kicked, his fists opening and shutting like two beating hearts. I stood, holding him to my breast, contemplating that patch of shade. One of my feet had fallen asleep. The baby pummeled my ribs with his hands, his knees, his head. I went to the front door, stepped outside. The baby stopped crying. I carried him across the grass to the shady spot underneath the bushes.

From the easy chair I could see the baby. Although his mouth was open, he did not seem to be crying. I closed my eyes for a moment and took in the now unfamiliar sound of my own breathing, like sandpaper slowly defining a scrap of wood. When I opened my eyes, the baby looked as though he belonged in the silence of the shade, his white diaper and t-shirt almost glowing, his arms and legs swaying in the air. A cloak of sunlight warmed my legs. I dissolved little by little into the palm of the chair, my mouth and eyelids surrendering to gravity, muscles in my legs clenching and unclenching.

Hearing the scrape of the key in the back lock, I sighed and pulled myself away from the quiet and the warmth of the chair. The baby was lying motionless underneath the shrubbery. I couldn't tell if he were asleep. I sat on the edge of the chair and stretched my arms over my head. It was five forty-five.

"You already finished your brief," I said, trying not to sound too pleased. Dishes clattered in the kitchen. I could hear the hum of the refrigerator after it had been opened and shut.

"There's no beer in this Godforsaken place."

The thud of heavy boots was followed by a violent throat clearing. Daniel's brother Stephen stomped into the room holding at arm's length a bottle of wine. "Since when did Daniel start drinking Chardonnay?" he demanded.

"Stephen, what are you doing here? Where's Daniel?"

Stephen studied the wine with suspicion, scratching at the stubble on his chin. "He had an emergency, didn't he tell you? He asked me to come by and start dinner."

"Oh," I said. I did not want to cry in front of Stephen, but I couldn't stop myself.

"Don't do that," he said, not untenderly. He held the bottle of wine between us and waited for me to finish.

I dried my eyes on the hem of my shirt, then returned the bottle to the refrigerator. "There's scotch in the laundry room, behind the detergent," I said.

Stephen retrieved the scotch. He grabbed two glasses out of the cabinet, dropped one ice cube in each, and poured. "Here's to you," he said. "One year older and still here." He downed the scotch in one swallow, gasping and rolling his eyes in pleasure, and poured himself another. "Dan always hides the good stuff." He smiled on one side of his mouth.

Motioning for me to sit in the easy chair, he lowered himself to the floor, his back to the picture window. Daniel had told me that even as a child, Stephen disliked chairs. "He needs to be close to the ground," Daniel had said.

Stephen drummed his fingers along the rim of his glass. "I'm starting my own business."

"Daniel mentioned it."

"He did?"

"Yeah. He said he was your silent partner."

"Not so silent, apparently."

"Oh, come on. It doesn't count when you tell your wife."

"Is that how it works?"

"You know that's how it works, Stephen. Daniel tells me every-thing."

Stephen was twenty-eight years old, ten years younger than Daniel, but he looked like Daniel's older brother. They had the same severe blue eyes, the same sloped nose, but Stephen's cheeks and forehead were sun-lined and brown, where Daniel's skin was pale, soft. Stephen was a carpenter by trade, a timber framer. He had never been married. According to Daniel, Stephen had had more girlfriends than he deserved. I had never met any of them. The last one, an older woman with two young kids, had broken his heart. Or he had broken her heart, I couldn't remember which.

Stephen sipped his scotch. He rubbed his chin with his fingers, which were webbed with small scratches and cuts. "Where's Nick?"

"Out there, where it's quiet." I pointed at the shrubbery.

For a moment he stared at me. Then he strode to the door, threw it open, and crossed the lawn, covering the distance to the shrubbery in a few steps. I trotted after him, wiping my palms on my thighs.

The baby was awake, still watching jewels of light jig and jag as the leaves shifted in the breeze. A cord of drool had dried to a pale crust from the corner of his mouth down his cheek and onto his neck.

"How's my little hedgehog?" Stephen threaded a calloused fin-ger into the baby's fist. The baby started at the sound of Stephen's voice, arms and legs twitching like live wires.

"Isn't it peaceful here?" I said.

Stephen scooped up the baby with one hand, gathered him to his shoulder. Standing up slowly, he walked back to the house at a stately pace. I followed behind, watching the baby gradually let loose the full force of his fury. His mouth opened so wide it appeared that he had the ability to unhinge his jaw.

Stephen went straight for my scotch, which I had left untouched next to the easy chair. "Couple of drops of this stuff would knock him out for a while," he said, gesturing toward me with the scotch.

"Don't think it hasn't crossed my mind."

"Couldn't hurt just this once."

I held my arms out for the baby, but Stephen ignored me.

He paced in front of the window, the baby thrashing in his arms. I watched him from the easy chair. Five minutes passed, ten minutes, twelve.

"How about the car?" The pitch of his voice surged slightly. "Babies love riding in the car, don't they?"

"Be my guest," I said. "If you think this is bad, wait until you have him in a car."

Stephen looked at me in disbelief. I had to bite my lip to keep from smiling. He rubbed the baby's back, held him aloft, kissed his head and his wrinkled neck, whispered to him. The baby answered in gasps that soon bloomed into more sobbing

"Have you tried putting him on top of the dryer?" Stephen eventually asked.

"Doesn't work."

"Damn."

"I haven't tried putting him in the dryer though."

Stephen started to laugh, stopped himself, sputtered, turned away. I hid a smile behind my hand.

The crying swelled, symphonic. Stephen tread a path around the edges of the room, cradling the back of the baby's head in his palm.

He stopped in front of the easy chair. "What does Dan do?"

"What do you mean?"

"I mean what does Dan do when Nick cries like this?"

"He doesn't do anything. He sleeps through it."

"How is that possible?"

"I don't know. It's kind of impressive."

"What an asshole."

The baby's limbs whipped wildly, his cheeks the color of ripe cherries, his mouth a black hole of anguish. Stephen was beginning to look queasy, feet pointed toward either door. He tightened his grip around the baby to keep from dropping him.

"Make it stop," he pleaded.

I motioned for Stephen to follow me back outside to the spot underneath the shrubbery. The baby was already starting to wind down a little as Stephen squatted beside me, his shirt damp with sweat.

"Stick him back in there," I said, motioning toward the nest of pine straw and leaves.

Stephen gave me a quick glance before he stuffed the baby under the shrubbery. The baby was still yelping, but it was clear he wasn't giving it his all. After a minute or two of half-hearted howls and a last furious flexing of legs and arms, he was quiet.

Stephen had been holding his breath, and he let it out in a long whoosh of air that smelled of scotch. He fished a handkerchief out of his pants pocket, wiped his brow. Leaning over, he whispered in my ear, "Good God, that was awful."

I nodded and allowed myself a smile.

We could hear birdsong and the hum of insects and the mewing of the black cat. The cat had appeared suddenly next to Stephen, rubbing its head over his cross-hatched knuckles. Stephen shooed the cat away.

"Why'd you do that?" I asked.

"A cat can steal a baby's breath."

"That's an old wives' tale."

"I know."

The baby watched the waltz of light and shadow in the branches over his head, his eyes wide, mouth ajar.

"You can't leave a baby outside by itself," Stephen said, looking down at his hands.

"I know," I said.

"That was a crazy thing to do."

"I know it was."

"Really crazy."

"Yeah, I know."

"I have to tell Daniel."

"Okay."

"He needs to know. It's his son too."

"You're right. I understand."

Stephen looked up at me. "I'm sorry," he said.

"That's okay," I said.

Stephen reached over and patted the baby on the head. "Probably be a lawyer, just like his dad."

"God, I hope not."

Stephen smiled broadly, revealing two rows of delicate white teeth, perfectly straight. I had always admired Stephen's teeth. They gave his rough face an aura of refinement and vulnerability when he risked a smile. He stood up, still smiling. "Don't you dare move."

"I won't, I promise."

The baby waved his arms frantically and then relaxed, his breathing heavy. Stephen returned a few moments later with two glasses, both with a new ice cube and a liberal serving of scotch. "To quieter times," he said.

"Quieter times," I said. When we touched glasses, we did not make a sound.

Stephen drained his glass. I handed him mine. He nodded and took another swallow. He exhaled loudly, began untying his heavy black boots. He pulled off the boots and his socks and rubbed the soles of his feet over the grass. "Can I ask you something personal?"

"Sure."

"How do you feel about him?"

"You mean the baby?"

"Who else would I mean?"

"I don't know."

Stephen raised one eyebrow and turned to look back at the house. "Oh," he said. "I meant the baby."

So far, during our brief acquaintance, I had changed his diapers, nursed him, waited while he slept just enough to rest his lungs, and listened to him scream. I had listened to the baby's squall, an enduring, wordless litany of grievances, from the moment he had been born. I was aware only of the quiet I'd lost, not of my feelings.

Stephen stared at me. He rolled his pant legs to the knee and pushed his sleeves over his shoulders. He had a fine body, muscular and lean and tan from working hard outdoors.

"It's all right," he said. "You don't have to answer."

"Mothers are supposed to bond with their babies," I said. "It says so in all the books."

Stephen cupped his chin in his palm.

I tried to be careful about the words I chose and the order they came out of my mouth. "I haven't bonded with him yet," I said. "But I'm sure it will happen soon."

Stephen closed a fist over one of the baby's feet, regarding him with obvious affection. "How could anyone bond with a smoke alarm you can't turn off?" he asked.

I started to laugh. The sensation was like getting kicked from the inside. It reminded me of having the baby in my womb, of being myself and not myself at the same time. I had not laughed like that since before he was born. I laughed until tears streamed down my cheeks. Stephen laughed too, laying his hand over his belly, flicking his tears away with one finger.

Our laughter gradually subsided into sighs and shudders. Stephen reached over and brushed an errant tear off my cheek. I liked his hands, his knotted knuckles, his craggy fingers lined with scars, nails permanently stained the brick red of Georgia clay. In my periphery the baby quietly jerked and trembled. Stephen, his cheeks flushed— whether from the alcohol or the heat, I didn't know—kept his hand on my face. He spread his fingers over the wisps of hair that grew along my temple. His lips parted. I could see his teeth.

When our mouths closed over the thread of air that separated us, we crashed headlong into each other. It literally took my breath away. Even as I gasped for air, I gasped for more of him. I had forgotten how hungry I could be. His tongue tasted like medicine. The sound of his breathing overwhelmed me. I could no longer hear the birdsong, the insects, the baby. At the sheer pleasure of it my breasts, which had been slowly filling with milk since Nick had last nursed, tingled and released a surge of liquid. It seeped through my bra and bled in circles over the front of my shirt.

"You're leaking." Stephen did not take his mouth off my mouth.

I closed my eyes and kissed him until I was nearly sick with the taste of him. Holding his face in my hands, I slowly pulled myself away. "I can't help it," I said.

"I don't mind." He licked his lips.

The baby appeared to be waving at us from under the shrubbery as he stared at the leaves overhead. Stephen ducked his chin to his chest, breathing deeply like a man trying to center himself. His hair was thinning on top, like Daniel's. I wondered what it would be like to sleep with Stephen. I had watched him fashion things out of wood—he had built our cherry coffee table—and I remembered his dexterous hands. He would take his time with me. He would seek out the places I had kept from Daniel these last few months, and he would fit me to him.

Stephen looked up, smiled, reached for my hand. I let him hold it. I wanted to believe that later, after Daniel had gone to bed, I would come downstairs with the crying baby, and I would lay him on his blanket of pine straw where he would lapse into the quiet. Stephen would be there waiting, casting a flimsy shadow in the moonlight. From down the street I could hear the rumble of my father-in-law's pickup. Stephen heard it too. He untangled his hand from mine to wave as his father pulled up in the truck.

Stephen's father marched across the lawn. He stood over us, hands on hips, an unlit cigar in his mouth. His name was Arthur, but everyone, even his students, called him Pop. He was a high school shop teacher. Early on I had figured out that the unlit cigar was an affectation. Pop was fastidious about what he considered healthy, and he deplored smoking.

"What the hell's my grandson doing under a bush?" he asked in a raspy voice.

"He likes it in there," Stephen said.

Pop glanced at Stephen, then at me. "How do you know he likes it in there?" He leaned over, picked up the baby, and headed inside, muttering obscenities.

Stephen and I looked at each other. It was quiet beside the shrubbery. The shadows had lengthened, and the cicadas had started their sawing. Stephen leaned forward, resting his chin on his knees. I did the same. Neither of us, it seemed, wanted to move. I watched his mouth. I waited for it to open, hoping to catch sight of his teeth. I had begun to miss Stephen already.

After a few minutes, Pop passed in front of the picture window, dancing in circles with the baby on his shoulder. We couldn't hear anything, but I noticed the baby's arched back and the frantic pedaling of his legs and arms.

Stephen opened his mouth to speak, closed it, shook his head, and smoothed his lips together. With his thumb he worried a patch of stubble on his chin, making an abrasive, almost metallic sound. "Helen," he said at last.

Pop was back at the window, jiggling the baby as he swayed back and forth. When jiggling and swaying did not have the desired effect, he began pacing, writhing baby cradled to his chest. Pop's lips flapped open and closed, as if he were singing to the baby, or trying to talk him out of his misery, or praying.

To the east the sky was a rich and pleasing blue-black. The filtered light of early evening made me feel benign, pliable. I thought of the rubbish that might tumble from Stephen's mouth. Compliments, endearments, confessions, accusations, declarations of one emotion or another. I did not want to hear his voice just now.

Pop, framed in the front window, was the picture of suburban angst, his face harried, lips contorted.

"I think your dad needs rescuing," I said to Stephen.

"Let him suffer." He stood and unrolled his pant legs, first one, then the other.

Inside, a volley of sound rattled the furniture. The baby, hands knotted into fists, was intent on finding his pitch. Pop, for his part, appeared to be trying to drown out the baby. He howled and hollered. He wailed, his mouth stretched all out of shape. I did not see the wisdom in this strategy, because the baby was afraid of loud noises and far too young to be shamed into silence. Not that I hadn't tried it myself on several occasions.

I wanted to tell Pop it was a losing battle, but I didn't think he would be able to hear me. Instead I walked toward him, arms outstretched. He shoved the baby into my arms. I sank into the easy chair, raised my wet shirt and bra over one breast, and cradled the baby close. He lunged for me. As soon as he started nursing, the milk gushed into his mouth, choking him. He cried and sputtered and lunged again. After another bungled attempt, he managed to latch on. Soon he was slurping away, body shuddering in bliss.

"Well, I'll be damned, you've got yourself a regular fire engine," Pop said, looking around for his cigar. It had fallen out of his mouth.

Stephen found it on the floor in front of the window. He picked it up and handed it to Pop. Inspecting it briefly, Pop blew on the tip and inserted it into his mouth.

"How about a drink, Dad?" Stephen said.

"Make it a double," said Pop, rubbing his hands through his hair. Unlike his sons, he had a full head of hair, yellow-grey, the color of dead weeds. His disapproval of smoking did not apply to alcohol.

"Where's Daniel?" Pop said after he took a swig of his drink.

"Working." Stephen and I said it at the same time. We looked at each other shyly from across the room. I switched the baby to the other breast, and he attacked it with gusto, milk dribbling down his cheek.

"It's past seven. I've got to start dinner," Stephen said after a few minutes. He ambled into the kitchen without a glance backwards.

Pop wandered around the room, trying not to stare at my breast.

"Bigshot lawyer can't get home on time for his wife's birthday," he mumbled.

"He just made partner," I said, less out of desire to defend Daniel than out of a need to say something conventional. The baby was slowing down, his eyelids sagging.

"What's partner worth if your wife's gone off with someone else?"

"Am I going off with someone?"

"You tell me."

"Maybe I am."

"Write me a postcard."

When the baby finally drifted into sleep, I gave him to Pop and went upstairs to shower. I tried not to think of Stephen. I thought instead of sleep. I had taken it for granted before the baby was born. I used to sleep for ten hours at a time. I used to stay in bed until noon, stretched out, self-satisfied, between the sheets. A full night's sleep and an idle morning alone now seemed impossibly remote. Now when I slept I dreamed of sleep. Now when I woke I couldn't keep my eyes closed. Overnight my bones had become old bones, sometimes brittle, other times light, humming like harp strings.

I had not expected any of this, but Daniel had wanted a baby, and I couldn't think of a reason to say no. We had met when I was twenty-one, a senior in college. I had just found a job at a coffee shop where Daniel was a regular. He was popular with all the baristas, a great talker, a born lawyer. "Lawyers are the scum of the earth," I said to him, the first time I handed him his latte. He laughed so hard he dropped the cup. When I tried to wipe up the spill, he took the wet rag from me, wiped the spill himself. I scowled; his smile grew more radiant. His attraction to me was attractive to me. After six months of taking me to dinner and then taking me to bed, he proposed. I was about to graduate college with a major in art history and no practical skills to speak of, full of fantasies about my potential. Daniel was funny, intelligent, ambitious, sexually experienced, gainfully employed, and besotted. He told me I could do anything I wanted.

I stood in front of my closet. It was full of slim black pants and tank tops in earth tones and little sun dresses from my pre-pregnancy days. I couldn't fit into my own clothes, but I had thrown my half-dozen maternity dresses in the trash. In the end I put on a pair of Daniel's jeans and a clean t-shirt. I glared at the mirror. My face was fuller, more pale than I remembered. My eyes, petaled in grey, were blood-shot. Delicate lines edged my lips. I smoothed lotion over my skin, brushed my hair, pinched my cheeks.

Downstairs, the baby was nowhere in sight. Pop and Stephen greeted me with gruff nods. Pop waved a hand over his glass. "Hit me," he said to Stephen, who was wearing my apron. Stephen poured. Pop took a swig. "Damn, that's good stuff. Where'd you get it?"

"I found it in the laundry room. Daniel stashed it in there," Stephen said.

"Stevie, you're a chip off the old block," Pop said. "Cheap son of a bitch always hides the good stuff, doesn't he?"

Stephen pointed toward the front door. "Go on back out there with Nick."

"It's too quiet, nothing to do," Pop complained.

"How about enjoying mother nature," Stephen said.

"Nature in the raw is seldom mild." Pop eyed the bottle of scotch.

"Come on, Pop," I said. "I'll go out there with you."

The two of us went outside and sat cross-legged beside the baby. He was snoozing, nestled in the pine straw. Pop set the tumbler of scotch on the lawn beside him. He sniffed, wrinkled his nose. Picking up Stephen's socks and boots, he threw them over the bushes and into the grass.

"You get out much?" he asked.

I looked to see if he were joking. "I've got my hands kind of full with Nick and everything."

Pop took a sip of his scotch and gazed at the horizon. The cigar was no longer behind his ear, nor was it in his mouth. "I could come over after school and watch the baby sometimes, if you wanted."

"Are you serious?"

"Sure." He rubbed his eyes, looking slightly bewildered at his own generosity.

"That would be great," I said. I tried to meet his gaze, but he stared out at the street.

"When I was your age, Dan was just a baby," he said thoughtfully.

"What was he like?"

"Just like he is now. Talkative." He kneaded his hands together. They resembled Stephen's hands, tanned, lashed with veins. "Never did like getting his hands messy."

"What about Stephen?"

"What about him?"

"What kind of baby was he?"

He frowned, smiled, tilted his chin to the sky. "Into everything."

Stephen waved from the picture window. He looked like someone I had known long ago. I waved to him as if from a distance, trying to bring him back within reach.

Pop poked the sole of the baby's foot. "Look at the little fellow. He's quiet as a mouse."

Stephen came outside carrying two glasses and the bottle of scotch. He sat down beside us and pulled my kitchen timer out of the pocket of the apron. He smelled of chocolate. "Mac's in the oven. Cake's in the oven," he said, pouring the scotch.

"I'll drink to that," Pop said. The three of us clinked glasses.

"You'll drink to anything," Stephen said.

The scotch tasted like nothing I could recall having tasted before, except the inside of Stephen's mouth. I shivered, took another sip, my stomach convulsing. The baby jerked in his sleep and was still.

The air outside had turned cool. Stephen untied the apron and spread it over Nick's sleeping body, tucking it under him. The sky just above the horizon to the west burned red-orange. Fireflies hovering around the shrubbery blinked on and off like tiny bulbs shorting out. Pop hummed softly under his breath. Gradually moving one ankle until it rested against mine, Stephen inspected his cuticles.

In the half-light of dusk, night noises flittered all about us—melting ice clinking against glass, the rattle of insect wings, the huff of the baby's breathing, leaves trembling in the breeze, the buzz of a far-off lawn mower. When Daniel's car coasted past us down the driveway, none of us moved. We nursed our scotches as Daniel slammed the car door, dropped something, cursed. After he shut the back door of the house behind him, the night swallowed us up again. We sat, grass cool under our feet, amid the dim quiet and watched the line of tarnished sky above the horizon fade to grey.

When Daniel opened the front door, a rivulet of light spilled over the grass. "Sorry I'm so late. I've had a hell of a day. I emailed a brief to this client about five. Then I packed up and headed for the door. I mean I was literally walking out the door, and the phone rang." He stood over us, light from the front door outlining his silhouette. "I almost didn't answer, but then I thought, What if it's Helen? What if something happened to the baby? So I picked up. And it was this client. He was screaming at me. He didn't like the way I argued the brief. I told him it was my wife's birthday. He said he didn't care if it was Jesus's birthday, he wanted the brief rewritten. I thought about telling him to go to hell, but I decided to stay late and rewrite it, get the guy off my back."

No one said anything. Stephen moved slightly closer to me. Leaning back on his hands, Pop scanned the darkening sky. The cigar had once again materialized. It bobbed up and down. I took another taste of scotch, holding it in my mouth until it was warmed.

"I should have told the guy to go to hell," Daniel said softly. His arms were crossed over his chest, tie loosened. With the light glowing behind his head I could see just three hollows in the place of mouth and eyes.

"Shut the door, Danny boy," said Pop. "Light's too bright."

Daniel pulled the door shut with one finger. "Why are you all out here?" he asked, hunkering down between me and Pop. He wrapped his arm around my shoulders.

"It's quiet," I said. Stephen and Pop nodded and the three of us again clinked glasses and drank.

"Is that my good scotch?" Daniel picked up the empty bottle.

"It was," Stephen said.

"We've been waiting a long time," Pop added, draining his glass.

Daniel studied the bottle. "Okay, Pop, I deserved that. I fucked up. I know it's hard for you to understand, but now that I'm partner I'm supposed to bring in a lot of new clients."

"Son, I understand more than you think," Pop replied, glancing at Stephen.

"Stuff it, Pop," Stephen said.

Daniel reached over me, extending his hand to Stephen. "Thanks, Brother."

"You can go to hell." Stephen's voice was almost affectionate. He stared at Daniel's face, his ankle still pressed against mine. I tried not to breathe.

Daniel smiled at me. When I did not smile back he touched my cheek with his palm. "I brought you a present," he said, his voice gentle.

Pop snorted and seized my glass, which had a nip of scotch left. Daniel handed me a brown envelope. Inside was a stack of papers.

"What's this?" I asked.

"Resumés." Tipping the empty bottle of scotch to his mouth, Daniel caught a drop on his tongue. Stephen sighed and handed Daniel his glass. Daniel nodded, drank. "I called a nanny service, and they sent these over. We can start interviewing this weekend. You need some time off, my love. You need to figure out what you want to do."

Daniel lifted my hand and kissed my fingers one by one, the way he used to when we were first married and he would drive home from the firm during his lunch hour and spend it in bed with me. "I'm sorry I answered that phone call. I blew it. I'm an idiot. Please forgive me, my beauty, my Helen."

I could think of nothing to say. Apologies came easily to Daniel, more easily than forgiveness came to me. I wanted to close my eyes and sink back into sleep, into Stephen, into a state of forget-fulness. I wanted to be suspended in warm, salty brine, knees curled to my chest, thumb in my mouth, eyes closed tight like Nick's as his lips moved, making a rhythmic sucking sound.

"Why's the baby under a bush?" Daniel asked.

It was nearly dark. We sat together in silence. The breeze carried the smell of burning meat from a neighbor's grill. When the kitchen timer next to Stephen went off, the sound was like a saw blade on metal. It jolted all of them—Stephen, Pop, and Daniel—from their reveries. They looked around, confused. A lone dog barked, and several others answered all at once. Someone else's baby cried. The cicadas were trilling in full force. The baby, utterly still, did not wake.

I noticed a dark shape in the grass, on the other side of the shrubbery where Nick lay sleeping. It was the black cat. I held my hand out, beckoning for it to come to me. I wanted to feel its soft cheek against my knuckles, but the cat sat motionless in the grass, tail trailing behind it. The baby was so quiet I wondered if the cat had stolen his breath. Stephen shifted his ankle against mine. Daniel squeezed my shoulder. I thought I should move, but I did not know where I wanted to go. When I looked again, I saw that the cat was one of Stephen's boots, a sock lying beside it. I searched for the other boot in the shadows beneath the shrub-bery. I couldn't see where it had landed. I searched for the cat, but it had disappeared into the cool breath of night.

TIM NOLAN

At the Choral Concert

The high school kids are so beautiful
in their lavender blouses and crisp white shirts.

They open their mouths to sing with that
far-off stare they had looking out from the crib.

Their voices lift up from the marble bed
of the high altar to the blue endless ceiling

of heaven as depicted in the cloudy dome—
and we—as the parents—crane our necks

to see our children and what is above us—
and ahead of us—until the end when we

are invited up to sing with them—sopranos
and altos—tenors and basses—to sing the great

Hallelujah Chorus—and I'm standing with the other
stunned and gray fathers—holding our sheet music—

searching for our parts—and we realize—
our voices are surprisingly rich—experienced—

For the Lord God omnipotent reigneth—
and how do we all know to come in

at exactly the right moment?—*Forever and ever*—
and how can it not seem that we shall reign

forever and ever—in one voice with our beautiful
children—looking out into all those lights.

Sellers Motivated

For awhile the house
sagged on itself,
then new people
moved in
with teacups that chink
in a different key
from the teacups
that lived here before.

There is an innocent
pouring of coffee,
a holding themselves apart,
a surreptitious glance
into my garden
as though I grew
rare greens. How hard
will they struggle
to heal that house?
Or will the cat
they took in
rend the curtains
and rain pour over
the sills at last?

Improving the Neighborhood

Red houses, white houses, drawing our curtains
against the spectacle of each other
washing dishes and trimming the dog's nails.
Now and then we exchange news. Life's
gotten harder, easier, nobody this week
has tied a noose in the master bedroom,
or watched his bed flame on the lawn.
Nobody in a black auto pulls up
to take someone away.

Outside my window, mourning doves,
in their ritual, nod and bow.
I kneel in the kitchen
peeling back layer after layer
of a housewife's life,
down to the plaster and lath
of whatever she knew:
only marriage is safe enough
to contain the immense desire
with which we enter the world.
When I take up the carpets,
there's blood in the cracks of the floor.

That clothesline has always stood
between two crosses; back and forth
for a hundred years
someone has pegged out the story.
I want to see her serene and disciplined;
nobody is. We all wake often,
ice pick to the heart, with our daily list.
We envy the nodding doves.

The house keeps crying about its own boards:
think of my story, atoms, forests, oceans
sweeping the sand you gaze through

onto the street. How can you pass
over anyone's lintel
without kissing the floor,
thanking each thing that positioned its body
to make you a stair...her face at the window,
her lamp guttering there?

Cleaning the Basement

Coming to scrub the fourth corner,
chip loose paint off cement
stuck with old stones,

I wonder who wrote in pencil *ace,
yummy!*—and why? Yesterday,
pushing a broom into the struts

under the stairs, I clinked
on an old bottle of bath oil,
labeled in deco style.

Thirty years in this house.
I've touched the penultimate pebble,
flushed out the spiders,

the buffalo nickel, the boyfriend's
dime bag over the workbench,
hairpins galore. The old yellow

and blue layers, loved like frescoes,
shine in the scrub water, sauna smell
of pine shelving, a slick place where aprons

polish the wall when we turn,
laundry basket on hip. Down-cellar the dead
are thickest, so much wash to do

and during the work, so much
to think over. Lines of housedresses,
white shirts and underwear wrung

and pegged to the winter lines.
I think we return
to what we were thinking about

sooner than anything done. We were so
interruptible: maybe it's only the basement
we managed to fill.

Vertical

Perhaps the purpose
of leaves is to conceal
the verticality
of trees
which we notice
in December
as if for the first time:
row after row
of dark forms
yearning upwards.
And since we will be
horizontal ourselves
for so long,
let us now honor
the gods
of the vertical:
stalks of wheat
which to the ant
must seem as high
as these trees do to us,
silos and
telephone poles,
stalagmites
and skyscrapers.
But most of all
these winter oaks,
these soft fleshed poplars,
this birch

whose bark is like
roughened skin
against which I lean
my chilled head,
exhausted but
not ready
to lie down.

Bread

"It seems to be the five stages
of yeast, not grief,
you like to write about,"
my son says,
meaning that bread
is always rising
and falling, being broken
and eaten, in my poems.
And though he is only half serious,
I want to say to him

"bread rising in the bowl
is like breath rising in the body;"
or "if you knead the dough
with perfect tenderness,
it is like gently kneading flesh
when you make love."
Baguette... pita... pane...
challah... naan: bread is
the universal language, translatable
on the famished tongue.

Now it is time to open
the package of yeast
and moisten it with water,
watching for its fizz,
its blind energy—
proofing it's called, the proof
of life. Everything
is ready: salt, flour, oil.
Breadcrumbs are what lead
the children home.

LUCIA PERILLO

Job Site, 1967

Brick laid down, scritch of the trowel's
downward stroke, another brick set
then the flat side of the trowel moving
across the top of the course of bricks.
My father stepped from the car in his brown loafers,
the rest of him is fading but not his loafers,
the round spot distended by his big toe.
Brick laid down, scritch of the trowel's
downward stroke, the silver bulb of the door lock
sticking up as I sat in the car,
the kid in the dress. Newark burned
just over the river, not so far south
as the South of their skin—deepening
under the ointment of sweat, skin and sweat
they'd hauled from the South
brother by brother and cousin by cousin
to build brick walls for men like my father
while Newark burned, and Plainfield burned,
while the men kept their rhythm, another brick set,
then the flat side of the trowel moving
across the top as my father crossed the mud.
I sat in the car with the silver bulb of the door lock
sticking up, though I was afraid,
the kid in the dress, the trowel moving
across the top of the course of bricks.
You can't burn a brick,
you smashed a brick through a window,
the downward stroke, another brick set,
but to get the window first you needed a wall,
and they were building the wall,
they were building the wall
while my father, in his brown loafers,
stepped toward them with their pay.

Love Swing

The new guy bought it as a present for his wife
(this a story Jim is telling)—
like a love swing like I think of as a love swing?
Jim uh-huhs: she'll ride it Christmas morn.
So let us stop to praise the new guy's paunch,
the dimpling in his wife's thighs,
though when I ask if I could ride a love swing
Jim says, "I'm afraid your love swing days are through."
In case of fire, strike chest with hammer
and wind up all the dogs in the neighborhood,
while I zen out trying to remember the name of…ah…
not Leland Stanford but *Stanford White:*
architect of the first Madison Square Garden
where the famous velvet swing hung in his tower studio—
tapestries, sketches, photographs, a hive
of mammoth work and mammoth pleasure
all mashed together in one place.
But it was the swing
that drove jurors wild at the trial
where the killer named Thaw got off the hook
because his young bride Evelyn had ridden it,
laughing and kicking her dainty feet. And I think:
maybe everybody in America has a love swing,
maybe it's as common as a jungle gym,
a secret no one has let me in on
until now, when it's too late. And my next thought
is that I have been all my life a tad repressed,
I mean I prided myself on having been around the block
but I never rode a love swing. OK:
I've bought a costume or two at the department store
that also sells chopped meat and pineapples
where you hide the impractical straps and struts
between gardening gloves and a ream of typing paper
as they roll along the checkout's conveyer belt
where the bra gets dinged with grease.

But nothing requiring tools, nothing with such
ramifications: the kids pouncing on their bunk beds
while you're hammering away, I mean hanging it up
so you can kick a paper parasol like the one that Stanford White
hung from the ceiling: fiddle dee dee.
What about the giant hooks?
and Jim says you get two decoy ferns
in silk or plastic, so as not to get dirt on the carpet
and because you don't want to hang your love swing by the
    window
where a true living plant could grow.
The new guy bought it at the Fantasy Emporium
down by Pike Market, choosing the swing
over the hand-stitched ribbon underwear
sold in the boutique next door,
which cost a week's wages. Jim held out his arms
to indicate the way she'll hold the ropes
a posture that made me think of Jesus
forgive me for saying. But I'm so far gone
I can say anything: Hello Mister Death,
let's run this bar code through.
Ouch—
that love swing sets you back more than a hundred bucks,
but hey it's cheaper than the ribbons
and will give you years of sailing back and forth,
hanging from nothing but a graveyard's smog.
Mounting instructions are included
though they be written in Japanese,
and it even comes in a discrete black shopping bag
to match your—whatever you call it—
your robe your gown.

Fan

Little engine of barbed wire
and autobody, miscellaneous tunes
drifting on the thinner. Crystal Dry Ice
when the wires weigh down, snap in the snow
and the refrigerator dies. Not today, a day
born hot, men pouring tar on the grocery store roof
before the worst of it arrives,
you in a hammock, book in your hands,
a chorus you've never seen singing one note
over and over. You, stationary as a fan
on an office desk, blades turning round,
round as the grove of oaks surrounding the farmhouse,
the man in the window, sun finding
his shirtless torso, fanning himself with the newspaper
as something rises from the mown fields,
vultures circling.
        By late afternoon
the shift at the mill over in Walker, two women
will sit on a car's hood drinking beer. Boats
on the river, the fisherman casts his line,
the girl on the inner tube pushes away
from the shallows. Evening when lightning
will flash once at the ballgame, the birds, nests hidden
in greenery, calling goodnight to their secret lives,
the whistle, so public announcing the train's
coming and going, each engine of song
swelling, pushing the hours forward.
        But now
in the hammock, Mrs. Ramsay remembers a night
twenty years before. Mrs. Ramsay knows her son
will always remember the disappointment of this day,
such a long day, half a book's worth,
and when it is over everything moves quickly,

and those who had lived are soon dead
in the war, in childbirth, in the night, and none of them
saw it coming and not one action
was determined by any other though it was,
fan turning, blades flashing, little world, the lightning
over the dark bowl of hills drawing a sigh from the crowd
at the ballgame because it is in its moment, beautiful
and free of us, striking fire far away in the woods.

Days Like Survival

Beginning in the midst of things
that split or burn or tear the skin
with happenstance, this elegant, unkempt earth
of rust and dust, smashed cat and armadillo
roadkill, abandoned pickup trucks
blocking the berm. A fine scum of rumor and pine pollen
coats cars and sidewalks, spring's clumsy fingers
smear the seen with allergens: the predictable machinery
cranks up and body opens into morning
damage done and not yet done, the hector and the haze
of early. Open the kitchen window, wait for its
drift and settle; open the front door that won't lock
properly, walk out with calcium-deficient bones, a rising
viral load, testing degrees of never
that set the temperature as something more
than temperate. Pause now, breathe in
an air of joblessness, its daylong sickly-sweet
catch in the throat. Warm
chapped hands at the world, welcome spring
with floods and heavy snows
across the continental weather zone,
a lingering low-pressure system's states
of insecurity, far west of this here and now
awash with these azaleas' purples,
pinks, and whites, these late camellia reds.

The New Life

I woke in the middle of a wooded
trailer park (in the middle
of somebody's lies), lying mired in a muddle
about where I was, with nothing
I could call my own: no shoes, no shirt, no pants,

no socks, no job or occupation, income
none. Wrecked mobile homes
on either side hinted at ruin
come and gone astray, what might return
for dinner, bringing friends

and friends of friends. The earth dressed down
in withered grasses and crashed trees, pine straw
and rusted household appliances,
made a welcome for me, made a grave
to mock me back to sleep. Raw sunlight

ignited my dissolving bones,
buried me alive in my disintegrating
body. How long it takes not to move.
My tarnished-penny idioms discoloring
unfinished loam, knife-edged

and neverward, I decided
not to die that day, made my mobility
my theme: stood up to red-clay dust
and downed corrugated fencing, uncollected
with the other storm debris.

JASON SHINDER

When I Think to Call His Name

I will dive to the bottom of the hotel pool

and find my mother's hairpin.
With the mouth of a drowning woman

on my lap, I will add her breath to mine.

In the dark, I will lay the thin white sheet
of moonlight over the blue plums

of my wife's breasts. With the new planet

I discovered just when I thought
I was losing my sight,

I will love another man because

I will be a woman. Everything important
will never as yet have happened. Let it happen.

I will throw a match on the secrets

my body has kept from me and stand in the fire.
The people I have sawed in half will appear

in my bedroom mirror, getting dressed.

I Want to Kill the Moths

I can't say: sweat, and then skin, and then mom, and then speak.
No such thing as a sentence, it seems. No such thing as what's
  happening.
Moth under the covers, get out. Brown wings, hung on the lamp
  stand.
If the soul lives in memories then the soul is no matter to reckon
  with.
Forgettable. I cleaned the shit but didn't get it all. She whimpered
  in pain.
She said *Stop it right now*. I told her, I'm sorry. *I don't believe you,*
  she said.
The bedroom flowers are purple and green, flushed bright when
  the window
shows dusk on leaves. The big pillows are wet with sweat. The
  smaller ones
are smeared with ointment, nests of hair. I dumped dead tulips
  in the bathroom.
Put water in bottles on windowsills. dumped the white spray,
  tucked
pink buds of peonies with the last dark iris from a larger
  bouquet.
I do anything but stop. It takes all day. I tried to pull her
on the pull sheet by myself. Wish me good luck, I told her.
Luck, she said. I looked at her and she looked at me
and we laughed, and when I couldn't even budge her we laughed
  harder.
But we were laughing thinking we are losing this, now. Thinking
  gone soon.
I want to kill the moths. This afternoon at the end of the movie
where a girl danced with her boyfriend at a wedding (outside, by
  a lake, at night)
my sister started sobbing and gripped my mother's leg. *You
  shouldn't cry,*

my mother told her, *it isn't good for you.* When we told her
    laughing that this
was the wrong thing to say, she told my sister *You can get snot on*
    my sheet.
Wiser words of comfort were never spoken, I told my mother,
and she said *I meant it as comfort.* Sentences don't exist. The you
became her. Now everything's over. The memories are already
    leaving
with the life that made them, that never made them, it just
    happened, it's gone.

TOM SLEIGH

The Chosen One

The embarrassment of wanting to pray to God,
the demand that God give a good Goddamn

had made him pretty nutty by the end; a lifelong Marxist,
he took up with Ouspensky, then spent all his money

(and he had tons, all those years in the bank
when *Das Kapital* and the *Wall Street Journal*

vied for subway reading time) on learning Gurdjieff
Sufi dances, spinning round and round in an ecstasy

of sweating, chanting, his happiness making him
call you on the phone to tell you in a way that made you

wince that he loved you for your holiness, regardless
of your failings that he would then go on to list

in rigorous, half humorous detail. But now, he was dying,
and dying fast, and he was pissed; pissed at life, more pissed

at death, most pissed at us, his useless fucking friends,
hangdog, silent under his scorn, withstanding his tongue-
       lashings,

then withdrawing to email, messages left on his machine.
And through it all, only his little dog, a white terrier

named Constanza, escaped his vitriol, his mortified, lacerating,
self-annihilating rages set off, so he said, by God's hatred,

God's malice, God's need to get his hooks in you
and twist you and turn you until His bullying was satisfied.

And while he was saying this, his hand would drift down
past the bedrails and immediately she was there,

licking his fingers, looking up with complete canine
accommodation, the reassuring tail wagging undismayed

by the smell beginning to come off him. It was as if God
put the dog in the room to uncover his friends as paltry

Job's comforters, in an accursed experiment to show
how isolated death can make a man, so that only

a dumb creature could be avid in its love, rising up
as we fell down in the scale of his affections;

and how he gave himself to that tongue, its absorbed,
infantile bliss, the dog up on her hind legs

coming out of her dogginess to meet him coming out
of his God cursed pain: her tongue slathered

and slurped his pungently acrid,
irresistible salts, the soon to be carrion salts

that gave to him such flavor—he, her chosen one,
his skin and smell enveloping her in lusciously novel

stinks and savors, as if only now was he the chrism, the oil
her dog-hearted devotions had so long thirsted for.

Round

Somebody's alone in his head, somebody's a kid,
somebody's arm's getting twisted—a sandwich flies apart,

tomatoes torn, white bread flung, then smeared with shit
and handed back to eat—*I dog dare you, I double dog dare you...*

Somebody's watching little shit friends watch little shit him
climb to the crown of a broken-down cherry tree

and throw cherries at him: now somebody's pushing
somebody into a sprinkler, everyone's laughing, everyone's shouting

in that frenzy when a buddy's gonna get hurt,
gonna get mad, gonna swing and swing from the top of the sky—

somebody's falling through trees shedding leaves,
October light you can see through,

somebody can't read the menu, can't find his glasses,
can't remember most mornings his best friends' names—

somebody's racing just ahead of what it means to be "it,"
porch lights coming on, trees jumping out at him,

and that nameless smell, smell of the high school lunchroom
mingled with formaldehyde when somebody does dissections,

frog legs strangely human under the fine-edged scalpel,
keeps making somebody waken, not certain anymore

of what window, which door, voices fading to a spectral
whine in somebody's ears, eyes calm, clear, the starpoint steeple

piercing somebody's brain moving alone through mist, darkness, rain,
somebody's eye's, somebody's mouth cooling, hardening to bronze.

TOM SLEIGH

Pig from Ohio

If you're a pig from Ohio,
all muscle and gristle,
not knowing they're planning
to rend you into bacon,

what better place
to find a wallow
than this blue-black mud
where you can keep yourself cool

as you wait for David
from Williamsfield, Ohio,
Sergeant in the Army's
4th Infantry—

two thousand-
six-hundred-fifty-seventh
casualty whose shadow
gets swallowed

in the 16 acre, 70 foot
hole that floats
on the Late Edition's
verso: the pig squeals

from the front page
smearing on fingers
of subway riders
who hear the echoes

through earth-movers
roaring all day
all night to fill the hole.
David, last name

Gordon, killed
in combat
by an IED
blasting through the armor

of his smoked Humvee,
David, take these slops
and shove them
in the pink face

and lashless eyes,
the slung belly's
sensual repose—
the good-natured maw

spreads wide as the air
as it squeals and drums
delicate trotters
in the swine fandango

a pig from Ohio
dances in time
to its appetite
that knows no better

than to bite
and bite
through wire,
bones, cans.

The Dog in the Wall

They said that's where Lulu
went, that was the smell. Not
rats.

Fifty years go by. They say
Yes. They don't change their story,
it's true.

A low cement block fence around
the house, a collie dog bark,
four kids.

Not collie, but collie dog, Howdy
as in Doody, The Stooges on someone else's
TV.

A young man's house, the wall's 2 x 4
at most, the why of a big dead dog,
a shovel

to the head? It barks less then the kids
howl. The work site in winter,
all of us waiting

to move in, the dog's tail in our faces.
Propitiary, an offering? They laugh.
The dog

never returned—the old house too far
to run back to, the scent long gone.
The pawing,

clawing against the sheetrock
my ear touches. Squirrels? The panting.
The whine.

The Little I

Hammer out of the cage
the movie insists: banged blonde,

blocked highway the gorilla helps
wreck—look, Ma, no cloverleaf.

The chaste scene. The woman
born from the thigh

she is holding, the one eye
of the truck that becomes worry.

I'm not the Lithuanian accenting
Every threat, I'm not even

the foliage that spends itself
as expensive rubbish.

The tires squeal: *save the animals!*
Let property damage end it.

He beats his chest until it's shot,
until open wounds, O love, admit me.

BRIAN SWANN

Loneliness

Like a voice drifting across low damp ground
    it is always there. I have whole files
on the subject. There is nothing more to know.
    My name hangs like a sign outside an old inn,
a painted figure for illiterates, blown to and fro.
    Last night I had a dream of finally falling in love
with a girl I used to know but couldn't recognize,
    whose face gradually morphed into someone
I'd known years before that and put up with
    her crazy cats and pretentious lefty friends,
a child snatched away at birth by his father
    and taken to Germany, her sister and awful family
with fake aristocratic Hungarian names, De-this
    and De that, an uncle who praised Hitler, and a mother
who looked exactly like Eva Braun, who talked incessantly
    through a terrible overbite. This was what passed
for my deep and final love. There was no way out.
    So, today, I sit upstairs on a day that's dropped
30 degrees in July. I'm stuck. The sound of my wife's
    radio filters through the closed door. My hand reaches
down to pat the invisible dog, calm the invisible child.
    I try to think in a foreign language, one I used to know,
even dream in. The wind is stirring up trees to a frenzy,
    but the chimes on the deck are silent and still.
It must have managed to avoid them, somehow
    sweeping round, so it's the silence of bells I hear.

JANUSZ SZUBER

Entelechy

translated by Ewa Hryniewicz-Yarbrough

In tennis shoes whitened with toothpaste
Running next to a hoop steered with a stick
From the hill down the footpaths of Aptekarka park
I'd like to see myself today
Through your boy's eyes. Our shared shame
Under the duckweed of still ponds.
Above them, in that past now, the rusty sun.
Which of us more real? Who should forgive whom?
Maybe you me since I let you down.
So when you pass me busy with the hoop
I won't even try to stop you,
I'll let you keep on running.

Between Ice and Water

Accept it. There will never be anything else
Except this here. April snowstorm
Sweeps away the filaments of smoke, and then
The sun appears and melting ice
Drop by drop trickles from stiff cables.
Let's avoid misunderstanding
Stammer out this rapture together with sorrow
Between ice and water, in the hazy
Spring light when drain pipes clank.
Don't say you can't accept
This here. There will never be
Anything else in the hazy light of a snowstorm
When drain pipes clank between ice
And water. This rapture.
This rapture and this sorrow.

Everything Here

The gray building of a pig farm, inside
Grunting and growling, almost black doughy mud
Through which they slogged, in squelching rubber boots,
That wet summer abounding in frogs, they worked
By accident on this farm, not quite a farm, in a poor
Region of dwarf pines and junipers,
Partly withered, at the edge of sloping
Pastures and soggy meadows, over which,
Once or twice a week, border patrols flew
In the potbellied dragonflies of helicopters, everything here,
Despite the emptiness stretching on for miles,
Barren, nobody's, was filled entirely with itself,
And when you sat over beer under the roof of that
makeshift bar,
Without the need to prove anything,
All this had something in it that could never
Be trapped by metaphor.

To the Rescue

Think of a lizard as a spot of day-glo green,
insect-sized, though in all ways perfect.

Lost in this kitchen of chrome-souled
recipes for oblivion, he looks hard at me.

His skin, my skin, our heartbeats tight with
trauma, I carry him out where, tack-sharp,

two green push-ups, and a cool survey
of the universe, my endangered species

walks, not runs, leaving his savior
staring at two brown leaves pasted by rain.

The Garden

The riddle of the garden is the garden.
The hollyhocks, chest-high, their irresponsible profligacy.
The nethering stonecrop.

The wax in which the body walks.
The fragrance kneeling at the lily's mouth.
The story that is
the lily, the fragrance;
the peonies, their exfoliate hives.

The weavers in their close huts of wattle
hurl questions at the sun
which hurls them back, to the generation of the moon
and her pitted typewriter.

I have not suppressed enough.
The small teeth, white like teeth, like coconut
between teeth, the sand
mixed with pearls and blood. And bringing forth:
the body's liquor. Sweet or sweeter.

There is a typewriter in the garden
to record the riddle in its unfolding.
Its keys are of malachite. I am too short to reach them.

Declination of checkerberry, the horsetail fern in its seep.

A body shapes the taste my body wakes.

Inscrutable Twist

The twist of the stream was inscrutable.
It was a seemingly run-of-the-mill
stream that flowed for several miles by the side
of Route 302 in northern Vermont—
and presumably does still—but I've not
been back there for what seems like a long time.

I have it in my mind's eye, the way
one crested a rise and rounded a corner
on the narrow blacktop, going west, and saw
off to the left in the flat green meadow
the stream turning briefly back on itself
to form a perfect loop—a useless light-filled
water noose or fragment of moon's cursive,
a sign or message of some kind—but left behind.

Thinking about Moss

Outside a deconsecrated church
turned nightclub on Sixth Avenue remains
a thriving patch of moss, green as spring
even in winter. Tucked along the edge
of the foundation, it renews itself
imperceptibly beneath our eyes, proof
that people and their constructions change
more quickly than plants and less
predictably. We gather and disperse
under this pretext or that, flying
our beliefs like bright kites while the string
lengthens and then snaps. Which of us could say
how long that moss has lived there, sacred
in its busyness, absolute by nature?

Even if we stop to watch, we can't see
it working. Garbage men early
in the morning bowl trash cans down
the avenue in the milky light
as if aiming for a strike. Waiters
poise for a fervent smoke at the curb
before plunging back through the front doors
of restaurants. Street sellers of all stripes
hover like peripatetic hosts
torn between showcasing their wares
and consolidating them for a quick
getaway if the cops show up. Humans—
we jangle like bells with our need to be noticed,
we ring in our towers balanced on air.

Outsiders

Let the watchers admit to
the terror of being young,
and the writers set down
on blackboards their fear.

It is the people's right
to ask exile or blood,
the people's privilege
to eat the cheapest food.

While the talk of guns
worms into the dreams
of the citizens, every
schoolyard is the same.

Salomé kisses the mouth
horrible on its platter;
the prophet's hard eyes
flare in all our shadows.

The Soldier Plant

The soldier plant
is perverse. Common
to civilizations,
it is like nothing
else in Nature.
Blown down upon
the richest earth,
its seeds will not
root: nourished
by blood and tears,
they will not ripen;
even prayed over,
celebrated in myth,
imagined as history,
tended to a fault,
they never flower.

The Great Loneliness

Everyone had heard of the great Loneliness
but no one could be sure they had it,
it's impossible to talk about
and comparisons are useless,
like trying to judge butterflies by weight.
You could be folding towels still warm from the dryer
and suffering the Great Loneliness
or suffering falling short of the Great Loneliness
which is like the suffering of crofters
in 18th century novels,
there only to reveal some aspect of character
in the real players. You might as well
be lunching at the healthclub
as holding yourself together in a maelstrom.
You could be a boy who drove a rusty nail
through your foot and now must stay inside
listening through the screen to his friends play tag
or a woman fingering her pearls while
everyone talks about the adulteries of celebrities.
Maybe you only kissed the impossible one twice
for the rose bush to send its thorns
through your insides but still, no knowing.
And your friend, the expert, who turned her freezer
into a diorama of failed arctic expedition
and likes to stand under a waterfall
and scream, even she can't be sure.
There are tests, of course, autopsies,
an unusual hollowness in long bones,
a bubble in the oblongata
but by then what does it matter
when you'll never be lonely again,
that puppy who ran into the road,
it wasn't your fault, licking your face?

The Sixteenth Section

The house where I grew up burned about thirty years ago. It was situated a few miles north of Loring, near the intersection of two country roads, only one of which was paved when I was a boy. The one we lived on wasn't, and my dad considered it a major triumph when he managed to embarrass the county board of supervisors into grading it and dumping several loads of fresh gravel on it. Normally, the supervisors didn't pay much attention to a man like my father, but he'd been persistent, and in the end he won out.

The house and the surrounding acreage belonged to the sixteenth section, which was rented to farmers, to support the local schools. In our county, sixteenth-section land was put up for auction every five years, which meant that people like my father and my maternal grandfather, who until his death was Dad's partner, had to enter sealed bids on what, in local parlance, was always referred to as "the place." When the time to open bids rolled around, a certain number of relationships in the town and surrounding countryside inevitably got fractured.

*

Some of my earliest memories involve trips to Mr. Parker Sturdivant's barbershop. Mr. Sturdivant was a cotton farmer who only cut hair on Saturdays, and I was always terrified that my turn might come when his chair was empty. Bald himself, he showed no respect for anybody else's hair, and would just keep the clippers whirring until he got through with whatever story he'd started telling when you sat down. More than once I climbed out of his chair in tears, and I was not the only boy who did. Like most of my friends, I preferred the regular barber, a guy named Andy Owens, who had wavy red hair and delivered the Memphis paper. Though the papers were dropped off at the local bus station by a southbound Greyhound around two a.m., people usually got them late on Sundays because Andy drank all night long each

Saturday and was frequently forced to stop and sleep the next morning on his route. You would often see his truck parked at the edge of a country road, papers piled high in the passenger seat, Andy's head resting on the steering wheel. It was understood that if you found him like that on your way to church and still didn't have your Commercial Appeal, it was okay to open the door and slip one out.

Sturdivant's was the spot where men gathered to swap lies, sometimes stopping by even when they didn't need a haircut. They talked about the fortunes of the Loring Leopards or the Ole Miss Rebels, chewed tobacco and shot brown streams of juice into tin cans and Dixie cups, moaned about rain or the lack of it. Cross words were never exchanged. My own tears notwithstanding, I associated the place with laughter.

They were laughing in there one morning about the uses to which the word "public" had lately been put. My friend Eugene and his father Arlan were under the clippers, Eugene, as I recall him, a heavily-freckled boy of five or six, his father a slim, prematurely grey man in his mid-thirties, whose hair was swept upward in the style of such country singers as Ray Price and Faron Young. Eugene had gotten the better end of the deal: perched on the vinyl-covered board Andy placed across the arms of the barber's chair for boys like us, he cast an eye at his father, probably wondering whether or not Mr. Sturdivant was going to mess up and cut off too much. His dad, as everybody knew, was particular about two things, his clothes and his hair.

"Heard one of 'em the other day on the sidewalk in front of the Western Auto saying the town needed more 'public' parking spaces," Mr. Sturdivant was saying. "And then another one, that big old horse-faced fool they call McCarthy—"

"McCarty," my father said.

"Who cares?" said Mr. Sturdivant, who didn't like his stories interrupted. "He's just McNigger to me."

That drew a laugh from most of those assembled: my father, Eugene and his dad, and three or four other men. I probably wanted to laugh, too, but I think I can safely say I didn't. My mother had grabbed me by the ear once after I used the word "nigger" in reference to the man who sacked our groceries at Piggly Wiggly. When I asked her why she didn't pull my father's ear for saying it, since he said it all the time, or Grandpa's ear, since he said it, too, she told me that what my father and grandfather said was their business but what I said was hers.

"Anyway, McWhatever looks back at the other one and says to him, says, 'Yes sir. Deed we do. Deed we do. And we be needing more public park space, too.'"

Everybody laughed again. One of the other men said, "They think if you call something public, that means it's theirs. They don't know that just means it's ours."

Eugene's dad said, "It's not ours, either. It's the government's."

"You got that right. Get right down to it, there's not much the government don't own, is there?"

"Not much," Eugene's dad said, shaking his head.

"Hold still, Arlan," Mr. Sturdivant ordered. "I can't style hair on a moving target."

"You're not styling it, Parker. You're just mowing it." He looked at the mirror mounted on the opposite wall. "And I do believe you're about to leave me feeling a tad bereft."

Mr. Calloway, I'd noticed, loved words that started with be-. Bereft, bedazzled, befuddled, beguiled. I'd heard him say all those and more. Because I was so taken with the way he talked, I'd asked Dad one time if my friend's father had gone to college. He said, "Arlan Calloway's been to the college of tough luck." He told me Mr. Calloway grew up poor and that everything he had, he'd gotten the hard way, by actually going out and working for it. That impressed me at the time because I could see the Calloways had a lot more than we did. They lived in a modern brick house with a small pool in the backyard, and they had two television sets and a stereo. Mr. Calloway drove a new truck and his wife a new car.

Mr. Sturdivant stuck the clippers into the holster on the side of the chair, then combed Mr. Calloway's hair straight up into the air until it resembled pictures I'd seen of the Matterhorn. After turning him loose, he motioned at me. "Guess it's your lucky day, Luke. Time I get through with you, you'll look just like Yul Brenner."

On the booster board, I closed my eyes, unwilling to look at my image in the mirror. I heard Eugene hop out of Andy's chair and my father settling in there. As always, rather than leave immediately, the Calloways would sit and watch us get our hair cut, then Mr. Calloway and my dad would walk out into the parking lot together. Besides having been friends when they were kids, they were both members of an organization called the Citizens' Council.

"How about that Meredith boy?" one of the men said while I sat there with my eyes closed, Mr. Sturdivant running the clippers dangerously close to my ear.

"He's something, ain't he?"

"That boy better learn to sing 'Dixie.'"

"He ain't gone go to Ole Miss. Ol' Ross gone keep him out of there."

I recognized Mr. Calloway's rich baritone: "Ol' Ross is nothing but an ol' fake. I wouldn't be surprised if him and JFK are in cahoots."

I waited to hear what the rest of the men would say. I knew they were talking about our governor, Ross Barnett, and the president of the United States, whom my father had voted for even though he was a Catholic. At that point in Southern history the Republican Party had three strikes against it: the Civil War, the Great Depression, and Little Rock Central.

My father was the first to raise objection: "Arlan, I think Ross knows what he's doing."

Mr. Calloway laughed. "I never said he didn't, James. I'll wager he knows exactly what he's doing. It's you and me and the rest of this beleaguered assembly that's in the dark when it comes to that."

His comment seemed to forestall further debate—in the barbershop, he wielded that kind of authority. For a while nobody said anything, then one of the other men cleared his throat and asked, "Y'all think the Leopards got a bat's chance against them boys from Leland?"

By the time I escaped the chair, my head felt about ten or fifteen degrees cooler. I knew I shouldn't look at the mirror, but I couldn't stop myself. Mr. Sturdivant had given me a pair of white sidewalls.

*

Though the barbershop would later move downtown, around the same time that Front Street businesses began their migration to strip malls, it was out on Highway 47 in those days, sandwiched between Delta Lumber Company and Loring Auto Parts. On Saturdays the parking lot was covered up. People cut their engines wherever space existed, which in practice meant that you would often emerge to find another truck parked behind your own. As odd as this may sound today, when life in small Southern towns has picked up speed—everyone eager to rush home and access the world by clicking the Explorer icon—if somebody had blocked you in back then, you stood around and waited, talking to whoever else was out there, until the owner of the truck behind yours emerged from whichever of the three businesses he'd been in. Then you stood around a little longer and talked to him, too. To behave otherwise would have been unneighborly.

Somebody had parked behind our truck that day. In the last year or so, since I began to piece these events together, I've often wondered whether things would have developed differently if Dad had simply told the Calloways goodbye, then climbed into the truck and driven away. I say this because I have learned that in Loring County, in 1962, you only found out who was bidding against you for a piece of sixteenth section land if his bid was higher than yours, or if, prior to the announcement of the results, he went out of his way to tell you, which most people were understandably reluctant to do.

Since we couldn't leave, the Calloways didn't, either. My dad asked Mr. Calloway if he'd caught any fish the other day over in Lee Lake, and Eugene and I drew a ring in the gravel, then backed up to one another and began to grunt and push, each of us trying to drive the other one beyond the circumference of the circle. Eugene was a good bit heavier than I was, if I recall correctly, so it's reasonable to think he prevailed, though in fact I don't remember. What I do remember is that moment when, once again, I heard the word public.

"It's public land, James, and this is just what I've got to do for me and my family. If I can't expand, I can't borrow. Bank lends on the basis of how many acres you're farming. Benighted as that kind of thinking may be, that's how they are. You know that just as well as I do. In the end, what's going to ruin us all is labor costs. Time's coming when we'll be paying folks six dollars a day to chop cotton. Only answer I see's increased mechanization, but who's got the money to buy new equipment?"

My father was a tall man, a shade under six-foot-four. He eventually put on a lot of weight, so that his belly began to pull his back and shoulders forward: when he walked he always looked as if he was just about to step through a low doorway. But at this point in his life, he was still thin. I'd heard people describe him as lanky.

Though a couple of inches shorter, I'm no midget. So I can tell you that when a tall man is unwilling to meet a shorter man's gaze, he's got three options. He can either look past the crown of the other guy's head, so that it appears he's studying the horizon. He can glance from side to side, as if he's on the witness stand and eager to avoid the eyes of the DA. Or he can stare at the ground—knowing just how pitiful it looks when somebody his height does that.

My father availed himself of all three, first pondering a distant Texaco sign. Then cutting his gaze from left to right and back. Then hanging his head while his cheeks turned from pink, to red, to purple.

"No hard feelings, I hope?" Mr. Calloway said, while Eugene and I stood silently by, aware that something had just changed between our fathers but not fully understanding what it was, or how it would affect us. "I sure won't have any, one way or the other." He offered his hand.

For a moment, I thought my dad would refuse to shake it. There was plenty I didn't know, but I intuited that refusing to grasp the hand of another man, when he had already extended his, was a decision of enormous import, one with the power to alter lives—not just the lives of the four of us standing there, but those of my mom and Eugene's mom, as well as his sister.

*

What I couldn't intuit was the degree to which certain received gestures—shaking hands, smiling and saying good morning, opening a door for another person, slapping him on the back or throwing your arm around his shoulder—could hide, for a time, the riot raging inside. One night two men climb into a new pick-up in Loring, Mississippi, and head for Oxford to defend States' Rights. While they're there, insurrection erupts. JFK makes a deal with the governor, but the governor backs out, leaving the President no choice but to order in the troops, thirty thousand of them, before all is said and done. The air is filled with tear gas, and stray bullets fly. The next morning one man returns.

It was as if Dad willed the blood to flow out of his cheeks, so that his color became almost normal. He raised his head, reached out and shook the hand of my best friend's father. There in the lot outside Sturdivant's Barbershop, on a sunny September morning in 1962, he said, "We just won't let it come between us." Then he grinned and slapped Mr. Calloway's back.

ABOUT PHILIP LEVINE

A Profile by Kate Daniels

Although Philip Levine turns eighty this year, he continues to be one of our most energetic and prolific American poets. A working poet for more than a half century, he is still writing and publishing new poems, mentoring younger poets, taking on editorial projects like this issue of *Ploughshares,* giving readings all over the country, and teaching one semester a year as Distinguished Poet in Residence in the graduate writing program at NYU. He and his wife, Fran (they have been married almost a half century), have adopted an active, bicoastal lifestyle, spending summer and fall in Brooklyn, and winter and spring at their longtime home in Fresno, California. Now the author of more than twenty volumes of poetry, prose, and translations, Levine has garnered almost every award that our culture has invented for poets: the Pulitzer, the National Book Award, the American Book Award, the National Book Critics Circle Award, the National Institute of Arts and Letters, the Guggenheim, the National Endowment for the Arts, the Academy of American Poets, et al. The roll call of writers he has taught or mentored is a lengthy one, and he tends to remain connected to those whose early works he nurtured and whose dreams he encouraged. In addition to the family of three sons he and Fran raised in their "small California farmhouse on an enormous lot dotted with orange trees and with room for a large garden," Phil Levine has fathered a large family of younger poets spread throughout the U.S.

In many ways, it would be accurate to call him the great workhorse of contemporary American poetry—a felicitous description for someone born and bred in the fabled Motor City of Detroit, who is regularly designated America's "poet of the working class" and our only "proletarian poet." He first went to work at age thirteen, and, until he enrolled in the University of Iowa's Writers Workshop in 1954, he labored at a series of Detroit's factories, grease shops, and parts manufacturers while completing high school, and, eventually, college. It may be that this early, fundamental understanding of himself as a worker among workers is to account for his extraordinary work habits as a poet. Those habits transformed themselves into an unalterable discipline after Levine left Detroit for Iowa City. There he studied with John Berryman and Robert Lowell, part of a soon-to-be-famous class of young poets, including Jane Cooper, Donald Justice, and W. D. Snodgrass. After Iowa, he went to Stanford, submitting himself and his work to the bizarre and grueling tutelage of Yvor Winters (one of the many periods of his life about which he has written hilariously). By the end of his formal training, Levine had acquired the dedicated, thorough, and methodical approach to writing that he continues to practice today. "Whatever the drive is, we follow it," he says. "I've never known where I'm going until I've gone and come back, and then it takes me ages to see what the trip was about." His many decades of dedication to hard work and good writing habits stand him in even better stead now, during what he calls his "dotage." Though he's not expecting in late life to "stumble onto one of those great projects" like *The Cantos* or *The Dream Songs,* Levine keeps up his routines. His ongoing regimen of practice and repetition— the mantra so dear to the heart of athletic coaches—continues to yield well-built, memorable poems that he shares with readers through print, live, and electronic venues. His attitude toward his work as a poet is practical: "Work might keep me from turning into an ash tree or a cabbage or a horse's ass," he says.

Philip Levine was born in 1928 in Detroit, Michigan. His parents were Russian Jewish immigrants. Both traveled to this country alone, as children. He was a child of the Depression, whose family situation was further impoverished by the death of his father in 1933 when the poet was only five years old. What might have been a harrowingly deprived childhood was cushioned by the ongoing presence of an extended family—grandparents, aunts, uncles—who stepped in to fill the gaps when Levine's mother went to work full-time to support her three young sons. Adding to the tonic effect of being surrounded by "a strong family," were the robust and feisty working-class neighborhoods of mid-century Detroit which imprinted Levine's imagination from an early age. On his daily jaunts about the city, he encountered any number of unforgettable "characters," like Cipriano, the

Geoffrey Berliner

immigrant pants-presser, at work "in the back of Peerless Cleaners, / ... raised on a little wooden platform," and Stash, the drunk floor worker at Detroit Transmission who "fell / onto the concrete, oily floor / ... / and we stopped carefully over him until / he wakened and went back to his press." So many of these humble, hardworking people and their "small" lives—forgotten and unrecorded by history and literature—would eventually show up in Levine's poetry.

What he failed to learn in the classroom or at home, Levine picked up on the streets, and a cocky, defiant, near-brawling (though never violent) street style became characteristic of his poetry. "No. Not this pig," he asserted early on, and often. He accepted his anger at the injustice of the world, and refused to quietly accept that things were the way they were: not only profoundly political, but wickedly anti-Semitic, as well. Detroit of that era, Levine says, was "the most anti-Semitic city west of Munich." At an early age, he realized, "Something was very wrong with the world, and I was powerless to do anything about it." Those early years were made even more indelible by several "epic events" that impressed themselves on him as a young child: the outbreak of the Spanish Civil War, the growing influence of Hitler in Europe, and the material suffering and spiritual sickness of schoolmates and neighbors that came with the economic downturn of the 1930s. This confluence of events—bad and good, historical and personal—came together to create one of the most unique literary imaginations of the twentieth century.

Levine is, frankly, one of our most popular and well-regarded American poets. Decades ago, he liberated new territory in American poetry by focusing on work and workers. While this had been a significant part of Whitman's project in *Leaves of Grass*, Levine, writing a century later, had the advantage of the new Modernist era. His entire body of work is drenched (though invisibly) in the understandings imparted to the twentieth century by Marx, Darwin, and Freud. While Whitman gave us our first American portraits of ourselves as workers, carving the young nation out of the wilderness, creating a new culture from whole cloth, learning how to live together in our diversity, his essentially Romantic ideology required a radical revision by the time fourteen-year-old Phil Levine "discovered poetry" after an iconic summer, laboring miserably in a soap factory. Whitman's bountiful vision could not account for the complete breakdown of capitalism enacted by the Great Depression, and it had no coherent explanation for worker-on-worker labor strife, or the great wave of racism and anti-Semitism that swept through the west as material fortunes floundered. What Levine contributed to our literature was a continuation of Whitman's subject, but infused with a more realistic understanding of the hidden aspects of working life, the power of the unconscious, and the enormity of the historical, social, and economic forces stacking the deck against ordinary citizens. His personal experience of the dehumanization of the manual laborer in the era of mass production was probably what gave him that extra nudge up Mt. Parnassus. For Whitman the machinery of industrialization was almost completely marvelous in the way that it assisted Americans in wresting from the continent a new, democratic society, taming its wilderness, and extracting its rich resources. By the time Levine came along, however, industrialization's contributions to our prosperity had become more ambiguous. Levine wrote bleak, but beautiful, portraits of people who literally broke down on the jobs American demanded of them, leaving their minds, limbs, digits behind; who "dried and hardened," losing their identities, after being fired for injury or made obsolete through ever-more efficient machinery. For all the excitement of mid-century Detroit—"the epic clanging of steel on steel," the awesome, gargantuan scale of production— at the end of the day, there was no end of the day. The factories kept churning it out—whatever "it" was—24/7. And human workers kept filing in at start of shift, and reeling out, diminished, somewhat less human, eight hours later. The young Phil Levine was there beside them, not just recording it all, but suffering through it with them, as well. This early body knowledge has never left him.

Welding meticulous craft together with colloquial voice and ungenteel subject matter resulted in a new poem about work and workers that no one else has yet replicated. Even while Levine's poems remained connected to an aerie past of English-language poetry through their insistence on formal excellence, they broke every other rule in the book. Although he wrote his first poems in traditional metrics, and later in elegant syllabics, his most identifiable persona, from the beginning, was unwashed and raw: a voice infused with defiance, anger, and protest. Publishing his first poems during the height of the reign of the New Criticism, Levine matter of factly and unapologetically refused to accede to the insistence that the only "world" that mattered was the world of and in the poem: "No. Not this pig."

Conscientiously anti-fascist from a young age, he progressed to an identification with anarchism that remained an important part of his personal identity until middle age. Levine still carries about him the innocent spirit of an early anarchist whose politics and hopes are futile, but whose intentions are pure. His insights and identifications—sometimes outrageously leftist, usually outrageously comical—almost always appear wholly formed and pure of heart, and his frequent indictments of everything from politicians and governments to the choices made by other poets seem free of personal rancor. Whatever he may be wracked with, it is not guilt: he calls it as he sees it with no overtones of apology or insecurity. This has been a strength of his teaching, as well as a hardship for some of those who made their way to his classroom.

A significant part of Levine's reputation resides in his teaching. He taught creative writing and literature at Fresno State University for almost thirty years, and has served as visiting writer at dozens of other schools. Even now, when he might be taking it deservedly easy, he serves on the graduate creative writing faculty of NYU. Perhaps it is his inner anarchist that will not allow him to give a poor poem a break. There are legions of stories (surely not all apocryphal) that demonstrate his challenging pedagogy. At Columbia University's School of the Arts in the late 1970s, he was rumored to have reduced every member of his graduate workshop to public tears, the men breaking first. It's a tactic he may have learned from his beloved mentor, John Berryman, who encouraged him by his own example in the classroom:

> His voice is there ... when I teach, urging me to say the truth no matter how painful a situation I may create, to say it with precision and in good spirits, never in rancor, and always to remember Blake's words (a couplet John loved to quote): 'A truth that's told with bad intent / Beats all the Lies you can invent.'

Like many who have suffered early, traumatic loss, Levine's tough love approach to teaching is tempered with tenderness. For every poet who has been discouraged or wounded by his forthright assessment of their fledgling efforts, there are many more who have flourished under his editorial gaze, and reared back at him, demanding more. Those precocious young poets—Larry Levis comes immediately to mind—have recognized Levine's challenges as a kind of confidence in their undiscovered abilities, and a invitation to join him in the shared enterprise of a life of poetry.

The rapidly expanding field of trauma studies has yet to discover Levine's poetry. Although he has written less about the early death of his father than about other subjects, his work remains marked by the impact of this early assault. It is a juicy irony, waiting to be remarked upon, that the honorary poet laureate of Detroit and Fresno, lavishly praised for the indelible portraits of both places that he has created in his poems, is not most accurately described as a poet of place. Rather, the primary energies of his poems reside in the psychological worlds of people being acted upon by forces greater themselves. Frequently, they succumb; other times, they pitch themselves into a battle they have no chance of winning. "I'm afraid we live at the mercy of a power," Levine has said, "maybe a God, without mercy." Such an outlook makes sense for him. The god of trauma is a merciless god, responsible for disappearing the young fathers of five year old poets and allowing the Holocaust. Although place and setting help to define and memorialize the characters in his poems, and their narrative situations, ultimately Levine is and always has been concerned with something less concrete:

> *When I closed my eyes and looked back into the past, I did not see the blazing color of the forges of nightmare or the torn faces of the workers. I didn't hear the deafening ring of metal on metal, or catch under everything the sweet stink of decay... Instead I was myself in the company of men and women of enormous sensitivity, delicacy, consideration. I saw us touching each other emotionally and physically, hands upon shoulders, across backs, faces pressed to faces. We spoke to each other out of the deepest centers of our need, and we listened. In those terrible places designed to rob us of our bodies and our spirits, we sustained each other.*

That Levine has retained both his body and his spirit for almost eighty years is a cause for celebration. We have no right to expect someone who has contributed so much and for so long to our literature and our community of writers to continue laboring at his age. But he does continue. He is still at work. The job is not yet over.

Kate Daniels teaches at Vanderbilt University and is completing her fourth collection of poems, My Poverty.

POSTSCRIPTS

ZACHARIS AWARD *Ploughshares* is pleased to present Ander Monson with the seventeenth annual John C. Zacharis First Book Award for his story collection *Other Electricities* (Sarabande, 2005). The $1,500 award, which is named after Emerson College's former president, honors the best debut book by a *Ploughshares* writer, alternating annually between poetry and fiction.

This year's judge was novelist and memoirist DeWitt Henry, the Founding Editor and Interim Director/Editor-in-Chief of *Ploughshares.* In choosing the collection, Henry said: "Monson's stunning stories move 'from a world of hard but sparse facts to a storyscape of soft, fulfilling fictions.' He writes with distinctive whimsy and obsession, earning moments of inevitable, surprising beauty. At the center of everything is the 'radio amateur,' a meditative youth in Michigan's upper peninsula, whose father is withdrawn into a world of ham radio, whose mother has vanished, and whose older brother is armless and aphasiac. Around him gather stories of friends and town-folk that center on absence, loneliness, energy, causation, and magic. 'Everything in Michigan is due to saws or mines or bombs or Vietnam.... There's something unnatural, unbalanced, like an equation. Something to be righted. Solved.' Monson's prose is always charged and arresting as he plays with post-modern structures as deftly as Stuart Dybek, William Gass, and the hypertext innovator, William Joyce."

Ander Monson's recent publications include *The Believer, A Public Space,* and *Pinch.* He won the Graywolf Press Nonfiction Prize for *Neck Deep and Other Predicaments* (2006), Tupelo Press Editor's Prize for his poems, *Vacationland* (2004), the World's Best Short-Story Contest from *The Southeast Review* (2004) and the Annie Dillard Award in Creative Nonfiction from *The Bellingham Review* (2002).

Born in Ann Arbor, Michigan, Monson was raised primarily in Michigan's Upper Peninsula. His mother died when he was seven.

Then he spent several years in Saudi Arabia, where his father taught Economics and worked as an economic consultant for the Saudi government through the United States government. Monson's childhood ambition, influenced by television's *LA Law,* was to be a lawyer or judge. He had an early interest in reading.

Stan Krohmer

He went to Houghton High School for a year in Michigan, "punctuated by minor delinquency" before his family moved to Saudi Arabia. As a student he was "kinda dorky, playing the bassoon, making a bunch of crappy stuff in shop, but also pretty invested in the world of electronic bulletin boards and hacker culture and phone phreaking." Since Arabia didn't have English-speaking schools beyond ninth grade, the U.S. government sent him to boarding school at Cranbrook, in Bloomfield Hills, Michigan. There he "loved the classes, sang choir, played bassoon for a while, did well, took English, read good books, but also spent a lot of time doing illegal things online or in person, and ended out being expelled (well, asked to leave on threat of expulsion) four months before I would have graduated." He had been planning to do computer science or experimental physics at Rice up until that point, but thanks to the expulsion, Rice's offer was revoked, and instead, he went to Michigan Tech, then transferred to Knox College, "which is where writing and I met up." Graduating from Knox, he went on for his M.A. in Literature at Iowa State University, and then to the University of Alabama for an M.F.A.

Over time he was worked odd jobs. "Worst was as a janitor for McLain State Park in Upper Michigan, where I cleaned up vomit from babies and drunks and leaned to drive stick shift on a trash truck which I accidentlally rammed into a shelter and was nearly fired for." He also served as copyeditor for a textbook publisher; designer for the University of Alabama Press and others; and editor of *Black Warrior Review.*

His first real publication, a story in *Pleiades,* came when he was a Junior at Knox. Soon after that he won an AWP Intro Award for a poem, which came out in *Willow Springs.* He originally finished *Other Electricities,* his M.F.A. thesis at University of Alabama, as a trilogy. Unable to find an agent, he sent it out himself, but editors found it "too estoteric or too poetric." He tried it in the AWP fiction, nonfiction, poetry contests. Finally when it was runner-up for Sarabande's Mary McCarthy prize, the Sarabande editors asked for another look, and it was picked up. He explains "I worked heavily with Kirby Gann, my kickass editor there, to find its shape, even as they toned down some of the more experimental elements in the editorial and production process (for starters, their design is significantly less visual than mine was)."

Among his mentors, Monson singles out Robin Metz at Knox, and Sandy Huss and Michael Martone at the University of Alabama.

When Monson founded the online magazine, *DIAGRAM*, in 2000, he had been editing, launching, and designing literary magazines for years. But as the editor of *Black Warrior Review*, he had grown frustrated with the large staff and the conservatism of collective editing. He grew interested in "the visual aspects of text and combining visuals with text." Collecting pre-1960 dictionaries, he played around with cutting illustrations out and scanning and manipulating them, and was struck by "the beauty and oddity of a lot of the diagrammatic illustrations, especially when removed their context." In starting *DIAGRAM*, he wanted to do something different, and offer a venue "for publishing edgier, genre-promiscuous work and work that incorporated visuals."

Monson teaches fiction, nonfiction, and poetry at Grand Valley State University, editing *DIAGRAM* and the New Michigan Press. He has just finished a second poetry collection, *The Available World*, that is looking for a home, and is working on a novel, new essays, and stories. He lives in Grand Rapids, Michigan, with his wife, Megan, and three cats.

SUBSCRIBERS Please note that on occasion we exchange mailing lists with other literary magazines and organizations. If you would like your name excluded from these exchanges, simply send us a letter or e-mail message stating so. Our e-mail address is pshares@emerson.edu. Also, please inform us of any address changes with as much advance notice as possible. The post office usually will not forward bulk mail.

BOOKSHELF

Books Recommended by Our Staff Editors

Epistles, *poems by Mark Jarman,* (Sarabande): Prized for his achievements in metrical verse and his deft deployment of English prosody, Mark Jarman turns, in Epistles, to the prose poem for this series of thirty dramatic monologues. Jarman's explicit titular reference to the Apostolic letters of Paul lays the groundwork for an exhilarating experiment in this humble form. Paul's statement "For we walk by faith not by sight" (2 Cor. 5:7) catalyzes Jarman's narrators—elevated and plainspoken—to investigate religious belief and skepticism, body and spirit.

Lest loftiness prevail, Jarman brings great wit and good humor to his serious subjects, leavening gravity with self-mockery ("Recently I learned that God no longer delighted in my existence") and popular culture. Echoing Leviticus, the narrator of "Each of us at the community service center" declares: "In the community service center, razor wire, TV, the smoke of cigarettes joined in a single hovering body—these unite us. We have learned to love one another as ourselves. We have learned cookery, cosmetology, creative writing, accounting." The narrator of a related poem, "If we drive to the meeting with the speakers blasting," again satirizes our efforts to rehabilitate ourselves. Towards the end of the poem, the speaker makes a discovery. "It's like those group things in the '60s. And knowing my partner is old enough to remember, I open my mouth. But she is praying. Her eyes tell me. They are open and focused in the act of prayer. And I can see what she is praying to, and stop. She is praying to the God in me." Here, Jarman yokes east and west by conjuring the traditional Nepalese word of greeting and parting, "Namaste," which translates to "the god in me salutes the god in you."

Jarman makes excellent use of the parallelism familiar in Biblical expression and thought. The book opens with "If I were Paul," a monologue in which five single-sentence paragraphs begin with the anaphoric command, "Consider." A marvelous catalogue of human desire, "One wants, the other wants" showcases Jarman's witty and compassionate take on human nature. "One wants to describe the plots of novels, the other wants to eat dinner. One wants to list the steps for assembly, the other shouts at the racket outside. One wants to pray, the other plans the week's menu. One says just a minute. One says you haven't heard a thing I've said." Characterized by potent anaphora, the poem "On the island of the pure in heart" references the Beatitudes and the promises made in the Old Testament to the chosen people. To the modern-day spiritual seeker, island after island disappoints with the exception of one: "On the island of the merciful, we obtained mercy." The poem ends with the following: "On the island of the peacemakers, we depleted our numbers by hand-to-hand combat, until there were only two of us— a soul and a body. // Even as they urged us to depart, on the island of the persecuted, they begged us to stay." The kingdom of heaven, an archipelago of contentious islands, offers little in the way of conventional consolations save "mercy."

Towards the end of the collection, one speaker argues that we must reconcile ourselves to a "promiscuous" God, an especially compelling metaphor. "There is nothing to be done but to enjoy vicariously the fact that, at every moment, God is with a lover, throwing his head back, wailing like a woman giving birth." The simile that commingles male and female, giving birth and making love, locates God in the "bodies" of all animate creatures. Mark Jarman's narrators offer canny, erudite, provocative tableaux that "speak to our condition." In this book a gifted poet reinvigorates his most urgent concerns. —*Robin Becker*

Robin Becker's most recent book of poems is Domain of Perfect Affection. *Poetry Editor and columnist for* The Women's Review of Books, *she is Professor of English and Women's Studies at the Pennsylvania State University.*

The Pajamaist, *poems by Mathew Zapruder* (Copper Canyon): There is a famous story about John Lennon's visit to a London art gallery in the sixties, in which the Beatle was faced with a precariously tall step ladder leading up to a dangling telescope. When he climbed to the top of the ladder and looked through the telescope, he saw the word "YES" printed on the lens, which both repaid his risk and introduced him to Yoko Ono, whose work it was. *The Pajamaist,* a collection of poems by Mathew Zapruder, similarly requires and then rewards a certain amount of effort on the part of the reader, and, to me, convincingly stands out from the crowd of young elliptical poets of our time.

Like many poets of his generation, Mathew Zapruder is much preoccupied with the how of saying; he writes the self-conscious sentence of the era, brandishing the badges of whimsy, non sequiteur, and a mild surrealism. "In Canada" offers a good sample of the zany charm, and the intermittent pockets of a deeper sensibility one comes upon by surprise:

> By Canada I have always been fascinated.
> All that snow and acquiescing.
> All that emptiness, all those butterflies
> marshaled into an army of peace...
> ...When they come
> to visit me, no one ever leaves me
> saying, the most touching thing
> about him is he's so human.
> Or, I was really glad to hear
> so many positive ideas regardless
> of the consequences expressed.
> Or I could drink a case of you.
> No one has ever pedaled
> every inch of thousands of roads
> through me to raise awareness
> from my struggle for autonomy.
> I have pity but no respect for others,
> which is not compassion, just ordinary
> love based on attitudes towards myself.
> I wonder how long I can endure.
> In Canada the leaves are falling...

Frank O'Hara is audible in Zapruder's voice, of course, and enjambment visibly is the momentum-engine to Zapruder's unspooling monologues, but it is his syntax, once you get the hang of it, that seems most original in his work—it dictates the pace at which one follows, and it quietly zigzags to interesting places. In the poem "Water Street," an ode to Brooklyn, the lines wander down the page in skinny irregular William Carlos Williams columns: "My window / lets in I'm not happy / and I'm not / sad chimes / from the radio / the roofers listen to. / Above the streets / little leaves / wait for the key to turn." The slow unkinking of the sentence yields a steady sequence of pleasures, both charming and sober. "Water Street" ends: "Off the scaffold workmen are leaping / into the arms of lunch. / All day with hammer claws / they yank wet shingles / and do not look at the sea. ... / A shadow is climbing the wall. / Good borough people, / just as the last ceremonial / day of winter / leaves a wreath / floating on the water, / you brought me here / to respect relation, / to put truth / and beauty together / though sometimes I tear them / apart." The earnest substance of this conclusion is not an anomaly in *The Pajamaist* (whose title poem is ambitiously dark); Zapruder has not just a deft manner, but an inwardness which is sturdy and generous, a little reminiscent of the James Wright of a quite different era. —*Tony Hoagland*

Tony Hoagland's latest book is Real Sofistikashun: Essays on Poetry and Craft *(Graywolf, 2006).*

The Memoir and the Memoirist, *literary criticism by Thomas Larson* (Swallow): Unlike its parent, autobiography, memoir doesn't seek to tell the story of the writer's entire life but rather focuses on a well-defined period, event, or crisis. Nor does the memoirist need to be a VIP. What the resulting literary work loses in historical importance or epic grandeur, it gains in the poetry of detail and meditation. As Thomas Larson repeatedly reminds us, the true drama of the memoir comes from the tension between the writer's two selves—the self who experienced whatever story is being recounted and the self who is recounting and interrogating that experience from the safe (and not-so-safe) remove of time and space.

As post-modern as this enterprise seems to be, Larson is careful to draw the line between exploring the nature of truth and memory and copping to the cynical belief that nothing like truth exists. Despite the difficulty of keeping track of the changing versions of an event that emerge from looking back on it repeatedly or comparing one's memory to documents from the period or to a parent's or sibling's version of the same event, that's the very heart of the memoirist's project.

Larson applies his methods to some of the finest examples of the form, with exhilarating analyses of works by writers as diverse as Virginia Woolf, Frank McCourt, Mary Karr, Mark Doty, Dave Eggers, Andrew Hudgins, Maxine Hong Kingston, and Rick Bragg. The result is a book that deserves the attention of literary scholars and anyone attempting to add his or her own contribution to the genre.

That said, Larson suffers from a misguided generosity of spirit that leads him to lump Mitch Albom, Alice Sebold, and the students in his memoir group with the luminaries mentioned above. And he should be wary of borrowing the prose of the self-help movement, with its reliance on Campbell-esque "mythic journeys" and vague buzz-words such as "core values" and "codependence," not to mention his use of "suiciding" as a verb and "male death-events" as a noun when describing the propensity of the men in one student's life to kill themselves.

Larson also goes wrong when he expands his definition of memoir to include any nonfiction writing in which the writer interacts with his or her material, even if that material is rooted in current events or on-going research. The mere presence of an "I" doesn't make a book a memoir; and such a system of classification would leave the slot for creative nonfiction empty except for John McPhee's numbingly impersonal output during his Rocks in Alaska Period. Larson's suggestion that if you spend a year rebuilding homes in New Orleans, you should be sure to describe your own homelessness and reflect on "the meaning of displacement, or alienation, in your life" makes me want to scream: "No! Sometimes a book of literary nonfiction is not about the writer!"

Larson's indulgences when discussing students' memoirs (and sometimes his own) are more than offset, however, by the eloquence and intelligence of his close readings of the works of professionals such as Alfred Kazin, Mary McCarthy, Annie Dillard, James McBride, and James Atlas, and his persuasive final chapter about the role of the seemingly authentic American voice in contemporary memoir and our desire to be comforted and reassured in this, "the age of terror." As Larson perceptively puts it, "memoir's genius" just might be "to use its intimate-sounding voice, so culturally recognizable already, to cast doubt on the easy believability of that voice." —*Eileen Pollack*

Eileen Pollack's new collection of stories and novellas, In the Mouth, *is forthcoming from* Four Way Books. *Her textbook/anthology* Creative Nonfiction *(Thomson/Wadsworth) is due out in January 2009.*

The Flawless Skin of Ugly People, *a novel by Doug Crandell* (Virgin): In this debut novel, Doug Crandell reverses the age-old question of inner versus outer beauty to deal with its counterpart: inner versus outer ugliness. The novel compellingly reveals that physical ugliness (however this is defined)—because of the reactions of others—may isolate and alienate the "ugly" person, leading to serious psychological problems. True healing, of both body and spirit, is to be discovered in a reconnection with the human community, through the ministry of love and caring.

Crandell creates a strong narrative voice in his protagonist, Hobbie, who, from childhood has had a serious acne problem. Back in high school, Hobbie was subject to jeers like "Pizza Face," and as an adult, if he doesn't keep his face hidden, he risks someone pointing at him and yelling, "Hey, Clearasil." Cutting him off further from others is the burden Hobbie carries from adolescence when the Deacon of Washburn's Tabernacle Church sexually assaulted him. The Deacon assured Hobbie "it's okay, all boys are bad," but in Hobbie's case, his "sin" was revealed in his "face." Shortly after the novel opens, Hobbie is victim of a bear attack; the deep gash in his face, after being sutured, has left his torn skin "puckered up and pulled together, the edges revealing thick lips of skin" in the midst of his acne.

One of the strengths of this novel is that Crandell broadens the social and psychological dimensions of the work by including not just one, but two "ugly people." In considering the nature of beauty and ugliness and its various impli-cations for one's self and others, we have not only Hobbie, but his common-law wife, Kari. Instead of a skin problem, Kari has a weight problem, stemming from her own run-in with the Deacon, who raped and impregnated her. Different prob-lem, different genesis, but a common and shared reaction: post-Deacon, as we learn in flashbacks, Hobbie and Kari turned to each other for comfort, for a shel-ter from the world that had let them down, and once they became adults, they sought out jobs as tellers in banks in outlying, suburban areas, from one city to an-other—for Hobbie, drive-through preferred—to isolate themselves from those who might be revolted by their physical appearance. As the novel begins, Kari, weary of their continual disappearing act, and hoping to lose weight, has com-mitted herself to the Center for Healthy Living, a state away from Hobbie. In this clinic, Kari soon undergoes more than weight loss; she seriously reevaluates all the baggage their lives have become: "Weight doesn't matter anymore. There's so much more that's weighing me down. Your Face, my Weight, the DEACON, my dad, our fear, our love, all of it's so heavy I can't conceive of losing an ounce of it. How can I still feel all this bulk after losing so much?"

Hobbie and Kari ultimately do find solutions to their physical problems; yet these solutions are not enough in themselves, as Kari suggests. Instead, they both begin to realize the greater importance of inner healing through making connec-tions with the world they have, for so long, been cut off from. Ugliness in the nov-el rests mainly with the Deacon, who is ugly on the inside, however "flawless" his skin might be. Crandell makes it all believable, all real. He evokes compassion for his characters, but never pity. We root for them, and in a fine ending that rings in a strong measure of joy, we feel better for having read this novel. —*Jack Smith*

Jack Smith's stories have been published in magazines such as North American Review, The Southern Review, Texas Review, X-Connect, *and* Night Train. *His reviews have appeared in* Missouri Review, Prairie Schooner, *and* Georgia Review.

EDITORS' SHELF

Books Recommended by
Our Advisory Editors

Maxine Kumin recommends *That or Which, and Why: A Usage Guide for Thoughtful Writers and Editors,* by Evan Jenkins: "A pragmatic and wonderfully witty collection of advice on slippery usage issues. Even if you think you know it all, read it for entertainment." (Routledge)

David St. John recommends *Intaglio,* poems by Ariana-Sophia M. Kartsonis: "I only discovered this prize-winning collection earlier this year, and it stunned me with its rich and sensual language and complex narrative architectures. Without question one of the very finest debut volumes of recent years." (Kent State)

Gerald Stern recommends *Velocity,* poems by Nancy Krygowski: "These are courageous poems. The music, the language, which I love, is based on a terrific sense of things, and I don't know if it is the music or the knowledge which I most admire. This is a wide-eyed, assertive, wild, well-read, street-smart, edgy, loving, suffering, heaven-crazed poet. It's a joy to find her." (Pittsburgh)

EDITORS' CORNER

New Books by
Our Advisory Editors

Sherman Alexie, *The Absolutely True Diary of a Part-Time Indian,* a novel: In his first book for young adults, Alexie tells the story of Junior, a budding cartoonist who leaves his school on the Spokane Indian Reservation for an all-white high school. This heartbreaking, funny, and beautifully written tale received the 2007 National Book Award for Young People's Literature. (Little, Brown)

Andrea Barrett, *The Air We Breathe,* a novel: Barrett's exquisite, much-anticipated new novel unfolds in the fall of 1916, when America was debating whether to enter the European war, and focuses on a group of tuberculosis patients in an isolated Adirondacks sanatorium. (Norton)

Amy Bloom, *Away,* a novel: Panoramic in scope, *Away* is the epic story of young Lillian Leyb, who comes to American alone after her family is destroyed in a Russian pogrom. (Random House)

Ron Carlson, *Five Skies,* a novel: A tour de force of grief, atonement, and the cost of loyalty, Carlson's first novel in twenty-five years brings together two stoics and a teenage misanthrope in Idaho's Rocky Mountains to build a ramp to nowhere. (Viking)

Mary Gordon, *Circling My Mother,* a memoir: a rich, bittersweet memoir about Gordon's mother—a single parent who weathered war, the Great Depression, and physical affliction—their relationship, and her role as a daughter. (Pantheon)

Robert Pinsky, *Gulf Music: Poems,* poems: Pinsky's first book of poems since 2000 discovers connections between things seemingly disparate in this ambitious, politically impassioned, and inventive book by a major American poet. (FSG)

Mark Strand, *New Selected Poems,* poems: more than twenty-five years after the appearance of his first *Selected Poems,* Strand offers a magnificent new gathering of work, one that spans and celebrates his remarkable career to date. (Knopf)

Ellen Bryant Voigt, *Messenger: New and Selected Poems 1976–2006,* poems: In this collection, a finalist for the 2007 National Book Award, Voigt arranges poems from her six highly praised books alongside a group of astonishing new pieces. (Norton)

RICK BAROT's second volume of poems, *Want,* will be published by Sarabande Books this spring. He teaches at Pacific Lutheran University in Tacoma, Washington, and in the Program for Writers at Warren Wilson College.

CHRISTIAN BARTER's first collection of poetry, *The Singers I Prefer* (CavanKerry) was a finalist for the Lenore Marshall Prize. His poems have appeared in *The Georgia Review, North American Review* and others. He is a trail crew supervisor at Acadia National Park.

PAULA BOHINCE is the author of *Incident at the Edge of Bayonet Woods* (Sarabande, 2008). Her poems have appeared in *Agni, The Antioch Review, The Nation, Slate,* and *The Yale Review.* She lives in Pennsylvania.

STEPHEN BURT teaches at Harvard. His new books of poems are *Parallel Play* and *Shot Clocks: Poems for the WNBA;* his new book of criticism is *The Forms of Youth: Adolescence in 20th-Century Poetry.*

COLIN CHENEY teaches in the Expository Writing Program at New York University. His poems have appeared recently in *Isotope, New Delta Review, Fourteen Hills,* and *Runes.* In 2006, Cheney was awarded a Ruth Lilly Fellowship from the Poetry Foundation. He lives in Sunset Park, Brooklyn, New York.

SUZANNE CLEARY's poetry books are *Trick Pear* (2007) and *Keeping Time* (2002), both published by Carnegie Mellon. Her awards include a Pushcart Prize and the Cecil Hemley Memorial Award of the Poetry Society of America. Her poems appear in many journals and anthologies, including *Poetry 180* and *180 More.*

BILLY COLLINS's recent publications include *The Trouble with Poetry and Other Poems* (Random House, 2005) and a collection of haiku titled *She Was Just Seventeen.*

NICOLE COOLEY grew up in New Orleans and has published two poetry books and a novel. She is completing a book about Hurricane Katrina, and directing the new M.F.A. program at Queens College—The City University of New York. She lives in New Jersey with her husband and young daughters.

SALLY DAWIDOFF lives and works in New York. Her poems appear this year in *Indiana Review, Lyric Poetry Review, Subtropics,* and several other journals.

PETER EVERWINE's most recent collection of poems is *From the Meadow: Selected and New Poems* (Pitt). A recipient of the Lamont Award and grants from the NEA and the Guggenheim Foundation, he lives in Fresno, California.

ALICE FRIMAN's new book is *The Book of the Rotten Daughter.* Her poems appear in *Poetry, Georgia Review, Prairie Schooner, Gettysburg Review,* and *Shenandoah,* which awarded her the 2002 Boatwright Prize. Professor Emerita at the University of Indianapolis, Friman now lives in Milledgeville, Georgia, where she is Poet-in-Residence at Georgia College & State University.

JENNIFER GROTZ is the author of *Cusp*. Her poems, translations, and reviews appear or are forthcoming from *Southern Review, New England Review, Boston Review,* and elsewhere. She teaches in the M.F.A. program at the University of North Carolina at Greensboro, and is the assistant director of the Bread Loaf Writers' Conference.

JENNIFER HAIGH is the author of *Baker Towers* and *Mrs. Kimble.* Her third novel, *The Condition,* will be published by HarperCollins in May, 2008.

C. G. HANZLICEK is the author of eight collections of poetry, the most recent of which is *The Cave: Selected and New Poems,* published by the University of Pittsburgh Press in 2001.

EHUD HAVAZELET's novel, *Bearing the Body,* was recently published by Farrar, Straus & Giroux.

BRENT HENDRICKS is the author of *Thaumatrope,* published by Action Books in 2007.

DAVID BRENDAN HOPES is a poet and playwright and professor of Literature and Humanities at UNCA. His newest book of poetry, *A Dream of Adonis,* has just appeared from Pecan Grove Press. His play *Edward the King* opens in New York in May, 2008.

EWA HRYNIEWICZ-YARBROUGH's translations of Janusz Szuber's poems will be published by Knopf in 2009. Her work has also appeared in numerous magazines and journals, including *The New Yorker, The Paris Review, TriQuarterly,* and *Poetry.* She lives in California and maintains a second home in Krakow.

YUSEF KOMUNYAKAA was awarded the Robert Creeley Poetry Award in 2007. His most recent book is *Gilgamesh* (Wesleyan, 2006), a verse play based on the Sumerian epic and co-authored by the playwright Chad Gracia.

JAMES LEIGH is a writer, journalist, musician and retired English teacher who has taught at San Francisco State University and Pomona College. He has published four novels, plays regularly with two Southern California jazz groups, and reviews fiction for the *San Diego Union-Tribune.*

SUZANNE LUMMIS, author of *In Danger,* has appeared lately in *The Hudson Review, Pool, Poetry Flash,* and *Poetry International.* She is editor of the idiosyncratic www.speechlessthemagazine.org, and teaches through the UCLA Extension Writers program.

DAVID MASON's latest book is the verse novel, *Ludlow,* published by Red Hen Press. Other books include *Arrivals, The Country I Remember,* and a collection of essays, *The Poetry of Life and the Life of Poetry.* He teaches at the Colorado College and lives in the mountains outside Colorado Springs.

COLLEEN J. MCELROY, a Professor Emeritus at the University of Washington, has published poetry, fiction, and nonfiction in numerous anthologies, such as *Best American Poetry 2001*, and the *Oxford Anthology of African American Literature*. *Sleeping with the Moon* (Illinois, 2007) is her most recent collection of poems.

MICHAEL MEYERHOFER's book, *Leaving Iowa,* won the Liam Rector First Book Award from Briery Creek Press. His new chapbook, *The Clay-Shaper's Husband,* will be published by Codhill Press in 2008.

DAVID MOOLTEN won the Samuel French Morse Poetry Prize in 1993 for his first book, *Plums and Ashes* (Northeastern). His most recent book is *Especially Then,* published in 2005 by David Robert Books.

TOMAS Q. MORIN was educated at Texas State University and Johns Hopkins University. His work has appeared or is forthcoming in *New Orleans Review, Boulevard, Slate,* and *Best New Poets 2007.*

JOAN MURRAY is editor of two new anthologies: *Poems to Live By in Troubling Times* (Beacon) and *The Pushcart Book of Poetry: Best Poems from 30 Years of the Pushcart Prize.* Her most recent collection is *Dancing on the Edge,* also from Beacon.

TIM NOLAN lives in Minneapolis with his wife and three kids and works as a lawyer. His poems have appeared in *The Nation, Ploughshares, Poetry East,* and other publications. Garrison Keillor regularly reads his poems on *The Writer's Almanac.* His first book of poetry, *The Sound of It,* will be published by New Rivers Press in 2008.

MARY ROSE O'REILLEY lives in Minnesota where she works at being a potter, gardener and folk musician. Her first book of poetry, *Half Wild* won the 2005 Walt Whitman Award. She is also the author of five books of nonfiction, most recently *The Love of Impermanent Things: A Threshold Ecology.*

LINDA PASTAN's twelfth book of poems, *Queen of a Rainy Country,* was recently published by Norton. She received the Ruth Lilly Prize in 2003, and was twice a finalist for the National Book Award. From 1991 to 1995 she was Poet Laureate of Maryland.

LUCIA PERILLO's fourth book of poems, *Luck is Luck,* was a finalist for the *Los Angeles Times* Book Prize and was awarded the Kingsley Tufts prize from Claremont University. A book of her essays, *I've Heard the Vultures Singing,* was published by Trinity University Press in 2007.

MAXINE SCATES is the author of two books of poems, *Black Loam* (Cherry Grove) and *Toluca Street* (Pitt); she is also editor, with David Trinidad, of *Holding Our Own: The Selected Poems of Ann Stanford* (Copper Canyon). She lives in Eugene, Oregon.

LAURIE SHECK is the author of five books of poems, most recently *Captivity* (Knopf, 2007). She has been a fellow at the Ratcliffe Institute for Advanced Study at Harvard, and a 2006-07 Fellow at the Culman Center for Scholars and Writers at the New York Public Library. The excerpt in this issue is from her newly completed hybrid work, *Archangel.* She lives in New York City.

REGINALD SHEPHERD's five books of poetry, all published by the University of Pittsburgh Press, include *Fata Morgana* (2007) and *Otherhood* (2003), a finalist for the 2004 Lenore Marshall Poetry Prize. He is the editor of *The Iowa Anthology of New American Poetries* (Iowa, 2004). His essay collection, *Orpheus in the Bronx,* is forthcoming from the University of Michigan Press in 2008.

JASON SHINDER's poetry books include *Every Room We Ever Slept In, Among Women,* and a forthcoming collection from Graywolf Press. He teaches at the graduate Writing Seminars at Bennington College.

TAIJE SILVERMAN's first book, *Houses Are Fields,* will be published by Louisiana State University Press in 2009. Poems from it are forthcoming in journals including *Pleiades, The Massachussets Review, Prairie Schooner,* and *Crab Orchard Review.*

TOM SLEIGH's most recent books are *Space Walk* (Houghton Mifflin, 2007) and *Interview with a Ghost* (Graywolf, 2006), a collection of essays.

TERESE SVOBODA is the author of ten books of poetry, fiction, and nonfiction, most recently *Black Glasses Like Clark Kent,* a memoir which won the 2007 Graywolf Nonfiction Prize. She will hold the McGhee Professorship at Davidson College in Spring 2008.

BRIAN SWANN's latest books are *Snow House, Autumn Road,* and *Algonquian Spirit: Contemporary Translations of the Algonquian Literatures of North America,* all published in 2005. He teaches at Cooper Union in New York City.

JANUSZ SZUBER's work has been translated into French, Spanish, Slovak, Croatian, German, Italian, Ukrainian, Hebrew and English. A collection of his poems will be published by Knopf in 2009. Szuber lives in Sanok, the mountain town in southern Poland where he grew up.

DOROTHEA TANNING is an artist and writer. Her poems have appeared in *The New Republic, Poetry, The Partisan Review, The New Yorker, The Yale Review,* and *The Best American Poetry.* Her memoir, *Between Lives,* was published in 2001 by W. W. Norton. For twenty-eight years, she lived and worked in Paris, and now makes her home in New York City.

G. C. WALDREP's collections of poems are *Goldbeater's Skin,* which won the Colorado Prize in 2003, and *Disclamor* (BOA, 2007). He lives in Lewisburg, Pennsylvania, and teaches at Bucknell University.

LAUREN K. WATEL lives in Decatur, Georgia with her son. "Quiet" was the 2005 winner of the Poets and Writers Writers Exchange Contest in fiction and is her first published short story.

ANNE PIERSON WIESE's first collection, *Floating City* (Louisiana, 2007) received the Academy of American Poets 2006 Walt Whitman Award. She received a 2005

Fellowship in Poetry from the New York Foundation for the Arts, and was a winner of the 2004 "Discovery"/*The Nation* Prize.

ROBLEY WILSON has been a Guggenheim Fellow in Fiction and a Nicholl Fellow in Screenwriting. He has published five story collections, three books of poems and three novels, most recently *The World Still Melting* (Thomas Dunne, 2005). He was for thirty-one years editor of the *North American Review*.

STEVE YARBROUGH is the author of three story collections and four novels, most recently *The End of California* (Knopf, 2007). A Mississippi native, he teaches at California State University, Fresno, where he is the James and Coke Hallowell Professor of Creative Writing and the director of the school's M.F.A. program.

DEAN YOUNG's eighth book of poetry, *Primitive Mentor,* will be published by the University of Pittsburgh Press in 2008.

∾

GUEST EDITOR POLICY *Ploughshares* is published three times a year: mixed issues of poetry and fiction in the Spring and Winter and a fiction issue in the Fall, with each guest-edited by a different writer of prominence, usually one whose early work was published in the journal. Guest editors are invited to solicit up to half of their issues, with the other half selected from unsolicited manuscripts screened for them by staff editors. This guest editor policy is designed to introduce readers to different literary circles and tastes, and to offer a fuller representation of the range and diversity of contemporary letters than would be possible with a single editorship. Yet, at the same time, we expect every issue to reflect our overall standards of literary excellence. We liken *Ploughshares* to a theater company: each issue might have a different guest editor and different writers—just as a play will have a different director, playwright, and cast— but subscribers can count on a governing aesthetic, a consistency in literary values and quality, that is uniquely our own.

∾

SUBMISSION POLICIES We welcome unsolicited manuscripts from August 1 to March 31 (postmark dates). All submissions sent from April to July are returned unread. In the past, guest editors often announced specific themes for issues, but we have revised our editorial policies and no longer restrict submissions to thematic topics. Submit your work at any time during our reading period; if a manuscript is not timely for one issue, it will be considered for another. We do not recommend trying to target specific guest editors. Our backlog is unpredictable, and staff editors ultimately have the responsibility of determining for which editor a work is most appropriate. Mail one prose piece or one to three poems. We do not accept e-mail submissions, but we now accept submissions online. Please see our website (www.pshares.org) for more information and specific guidelines. Poems should be individually typed either single- or double-spaced on one side of the page. Prose should be typed double-spaced on one side and be no longer than thirty pages. Although we look primarily for short stories, we occasionally publish personal essays/memoirs. Novel excerpts are acceptable if self-contained. Unsolicited book reviews and criticism are not con sidered. Please send only one manuscript at a time, either by mail or online. Do not send a second submission until you have heard about the first. *There is a limit of two submissions per reading period, regardless of genre, whether it is by mail or online.* Additional submissions will be returned unread. Mail your manuscript in a page-size manila envelope, your full name and address written on the outside. In general, address submissions to the "Fiction Editor," "Poetry Editor," or "Nonfiction Editor," not to the guest or staff editors by name, unless you have a legitimate association with them or have been previously published in the magazine. Unsolicited work sent directly to a guest editor's home or office will be ignored and discarded; guest editors are formally instructed not to read such work. *All mailed manuscripts and correspondence regarding submissions should be accompanied by a business-size, self-addressed, stamped envelope (s.a.s.e.) for a response only. Manuscript copies will be recycled, not returned.* No replies will be given by postcard or e-mail (exceptions are made for international submissions). Expect three to five months for a decision. We now receive well over a thousand manuscripts a month. Do not query us until five months have passed, and if you do, please write to us, including an s.a.s.e. and indicating the postmark date of submission, instead of calling or e-mailing. Simultaneous submissions are amenable as long as they are indicated as such and we are notified immediately upon acceptance elsewhere. We cannot accommodate revisions, changes of return address, or forgotten s.a.s.e.'s after the fact. We do not reprint previously published work. Translations are welcome if permission has been granted. We cannot be responsible for delay, loss, or damage. Payment is upon publication: $25/printed page, $50 minimum and $250 maximum per author, with two copies of the issue and a one-year subscription.

NATIONAL
ENDOWMENT
FOR THE ARTS

masssculturalcouncil.org

THE
Rona Jaffe
Foundation
WRITERS' AWARDS

The Rona Jaffe Foundation identifies and supports emerging women writers. Recipients receive awards of $25,000.

2007 WINNERS

Elif Batuman
(nonfiction/fiction)

Sarah Braunstein
(fiction)

Robin Ekiss
(poetry)

Alma García
(fiction)

Jennifer Grotz
(poetry)

Holly Goddard Jones
(fiction)

WWW.RONAJAFFEFOUNDATION.ORG

SARAH · LAWRENCE · COLLEGE

MFA in WRITING

2007-2008 FACULTY

FICTION	POETRY	NONFICTION
Melvin Bukiet	Laure-Anne Bosselaar	Gerry Albarelli
Carolyn Ferrell	Kurt Brown	Jo Ann Beard
Myra Goldberg	Tina Chang	Rachel Cohen
Amy Hempel	Thomas Sayers Ellis	Stephen O'Connor
Josh Henkin	Suzanne Gardinier	Vijay Seshadri
Kathleen Hill	Matthea Harvey	Alice Truax
Mary LaChapelle	Cathy Park Hong	Lawrence Weschler
Ernesto Mestre	Marie Howe	Penny Wolfson
Mary Morris	Kate Knapp Johnson	
Brian Morton	Thomas Lux	
Victoria Redel	Jeffrey McDaniel	
Lucy Rosenthal	Dennis Nurkse	
Joan Silber	Kevin Pilkington	
	Victoria Redel	
	Martha Rhodes	
	Vijay Seshadri	

Write or call **Graduate Studies:**
Sarah Lawrence College, 1 Mead Way, Bronxville, NY 10708-5999
(914) 395-2371, grad@slc.edu or visit us at
www.sarahlawrence.edu/writing
Full and part-time study available.

Write without pay until somebody offers to pay. Mark Twain

James A. Michener Center for Writers **MFA IN WRITING**

Fiction • Poetry • Screenwriting • Playwriting

Upcoming and recent faculty

ANTONYA NELSON

ZZ PACKER

DEAN YOUNG

COLM TOIBIN

ANTHONY GIARDINA

AUGUST KLEINZAHLER

JOHN DUFRESNE

JOY WILLIAMS

DENIS JOHNSON

MARIE HOWE

Fellowships of $25,000 annually for three years

512/471.1601 • www.utexas.edu/academic/mcw

THE UNIVERSITY OF TEXAS AT AUSTIN

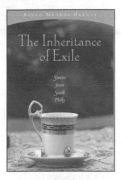

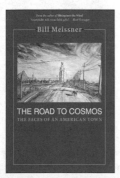

DeWitt Henry
Safe Suicide

Narratives, Essays & Meditations

**Henry is an insightful observer who is
also a prose stylist of the first rank.**
—Richard Hoffman,
author of *Half The House*

As with any flat-out wonderful book, a few words of praise cannot begin to do it justice. But here goes: *Safe Suicide* is elegantly written, edgy, touching, inventive, surprising in its shifts of style and form, and completely spellbinding from start to finish. Partly memoir, partly a sequence of interlocked essays, this is a book that works its way under your skin and down into your vital organs. It is really, really good.—**Tim O'Brien**

Safe Suicide offers an enthralling portrait of the life of the artist as a husband, a father, an editor, a teacher, a runner and a dog owner. DeWitt Henry writes with fearless beauty and honesty about his many, often irreconcilable, passions. Here is a life lived over time and the result is thought-provoking, absorbing, and deeply moving. —**Margot Livesey**, author of *Banishing Verona: A Novel*

Available January 2008

Red Hen Press
P.O. Box 3537
Granada Hills, CA 91394
(818) 831-0649 ~ Fax (818) 831-6659